AVEN ELLIS

Love, the Viscount, & Me

A Modern Aristocrats Novella

Contents

Acknowledgement

Thank you to Joanne Lui for her masterful edit. You always have a way of seeing through my words and finding all the things that need polishing and helping me find solutions when needed-while keeping my voice mine. I love you!

Thank you to my proofreader, Alexandra Morris for re-reading this book again, bouncing ideas with me, and catching all the things that needed to be reworked. You are the best. Thank you to Chris Jucis and Glee Cady for finessing everything with your eagle eyes.

To my beta team-Jennifer DiCenzo, the Beta Baes, and the SJFC girls-thank you for encouraging me, coming up with ideas, and being the most supportive friends a girl could ask for. You all are the best!

Holly Martin and Alexa Aston-thank you for always critiquing my work and making it the best book it can be.

Thank you to my ARC team and early reviewers for loving and supporting this story so much. I am so grateful for all of your support on this journey.

And finally, to all my readers. None of this happens without you wanting these stories and loving them so much. I'm blessed by each and every one of you.

Chapter One

I never dreamed that within the first few hours on the job, I'd be riding in the back of a black Range Rover, sandwiched between two fighting children, with two more seated in the row behind me, while their mother chats with me non-stop as we are heading out to the country to, in her words, "peruse mini cows."

Mini cows.

How is that even a thing?

For a moment, I ignore how Pippa is trying to reach around me and poke Byron, or Layla is arguing with Louis behind me, and focus on the rolling green spaces that whiz by the car window.

I made it to England.

I, McKenna Manning, have made it home.

Well, at least half my home. I was born in Essex but raised in Southern California. England is in my soul. It's the link to my mum, who passed away when I was an infant. I want to learn about it. About her. I can't wait to meet the long-lost cousins I've recently reconnected with, too.

With my newly earned degree in childhood development from San Diego State University, I'm taking a year off to find myself. My past. I landed a job as a nanny for Lady Rose Coventry-

Palmerston, whose aristocratic blood runs back hundreds of years. She has four children—Layla is six, and the triplets are four— and lives in London, in a glorious old house. I moved in this morning, and this is my first day on the job.

But on a whim, Rose decided we needed fresh air this Friday, and we all packed up and headed out to Northamptonshire for the weekend.

"McKenna is going to like me the best!" Pippa cries, interrupting my thoughts.

"No, she's not!" Byron counters. Then he turns to me. "Do you like *Shaun the Sheep*?"

Who? Who is Shaun? I flip through all the cartoons I watched on my previous nanny gigs. I can go through the Nickelodeon lineup by heart, and Disney, but I don't know Shaun.

"No! She's a girl, and she likes *Peppa Pig*!"

Okay! I know Peppa. The little girl of the last family I nannied for was obsessed with her.

"I like them both," I lie, knowing I need to keep the peace.

"Anyway," Rose says as she drives, "isn't the country beautiful? I know you didn't expect to be out of the city straight away, but if you spend the weekend in the country with us, I'll give you two days off next week in London. Is that agreeable to you?"

"Oh, yes, ma'am."

"Please, as I asked you before, call me Rose," she insists, smiling brightly at me in the rearview mirror. "Now, if you look up here, on that hill? See that estate? That belongs to the Rothschilds. Nasty family, I tell you."

"Do you like the farmer?" Byron asks.

"Who?" I ask, distracted.

"The farmer! From Shaun!" he says.

Damn. I fell into a trap. If knew Shaun, I would know this.

2

"Mummy, tell Louis the mini cows will be mini burgers and we're going to eat the cows!" Layla demands.

Louis bursts into tears. "I don't want to eat the mini cows!"

"Do they make mini milk?" Pippa asks.

"I don't want to eat them, don't make me eat them!" Louis screams, growing hysterical.

Rose continues her narration, oblivious to the chaos in the car. "Their daughter, Lady India, is *insufferable.*"

"DO YOU LIKE THE FARMER?" Byron shouts at me.

"Does mini milk come in tiny cups?" Pippa asks.

"I won't eat them!" Louis sobs.

"We're going to kill them and grind them up!" Layla cries gleefully.

Oh. My. God.

I have not been hired to be a nanny.

I'm the head of Chaos Control.

I quickly turn around to face Layla and Louis. "Louis," I say in a voice that is calm and soothing, "We will not be eating the mini cows. I promise you that. Your mummy is looking at them as pets, much like a dog or a cat."

"Maybe we'll eat them when they grow bigger," Layla says, a wicked gleam entering her blue eyes. "We need to fatten them up to make BIG BURGERS!"

Louis shrieks, and she laughs manically.

I need to keep an eye on this one.

"Louis, look at me," I say. He stops crying and stares at me. "I will not allow any mini cows to be made into burgers. Ever. I promise with all my heart."

He stops crying. "What about what Layla said?"

"Layla is wrong," I say breezily.

Layla scowls at me. Now I turn my attention to her.

"Layla, you are saying these things to upset Louis, and that isn't very kind, now is it?"

The car falls silent. When I interviewed with Rose, she told me that Layla has been "a bit of a handful" ever since the triplets were born.

The triplets are four.

It's time for Layla to have some authority and structure in her life. And for her to learn to be a proper big sister instead of a terror.

Layla scowls at me.

"Miss Layla, I asked you a question," I say.

Now she shoots daggers at me. "It's the truth."

"No, it is not. We are not eating mini cows, so you were saying something that was untrue. You need to apologize to Louis, please."

She folds her arms. "What if I don't want to?"

"Then you and I will have a boring time at the farm, watching the triplets play with all the animals while we sit next to the car."

"Why would we do that?" Layla asks.

"Layla," Rose says, sighing wearily. "Please stop."

"Because playing with the animals is not a right," I say easily. "If you choose not to apologize, you will not participate. It's up to you, of course. I will either play with the mini cows with you, or we will sit out. Which would you like to do?"

The car is dead silent.

"I'm. Sorry," she says through gritted teeth.

"Oh, that is such a good choice, Layla. Thank you," I cry happily. "Now we can all have fun with the cows!"

Louis nods. I can tell he's appeased.

But Layla?

She whips her head and stares out the window, her arms crossed, a scowl on her face.

I turn back around. My heart tells me Layla is still struggling to find her role in the family after the triplets came home. They've had two nannies during that time. One was Layla's nanny since birth, and she didn't want to cope with triplets and left. The next nanny preferred young children and left a few weeks ago to take a post with a family in Yorkshire who had a two-year-old and an infant.

I am nanny number three. According to Rose, she picked me because I was young and American and had a degree in working with young children. She said she wanted someone "different."

I, on the other hand, took this position because I love working with all young children. Coming to England was my goal, and I interviewed with several families. But Rose and her husband, John, were kind in their interview. They spoke to me as an equal. I told them my goal was to teach the children to be inquisitive and learn through play. I wanted them to have fun but learn to be responsible and respectful. I explained that teaching empathy, understanding, and compassion was important to me, and if the Palmerstons didn't agree to this, I wouldn't take the job.

Luckily, they did.

With the Palmerstons, I knew I would have the opportunity to live in London, which is what I wanted, but would also spend time in the country, which seemed ideal for my goal of exploring the land that is a part of me.

The part I do not yet know.

"Mummy! How much farther?" Pippa asks.

"Oh, my love, not too much farther," Rose says.

"Will Daddy meet us there?" Byron asks.

"No, my darling, Daddy has to work," Rose says. "But he

will join us for dinner tonight, and we'll spend all weekend together."

"McKenna, too?" Louis asks.

I turn around and smile at him. He grins back. Then I look at Layla, who I catch scowling at me before she quickly looks out the window again.

"McKenna, too," Rose says.

We continue our drive to this farm, which seems like an eternity because I have no idea where I am. Finally, we turn down some winding roads, and I see a sign promoting Wee Moos Farm. As Rose heads up the drive, we move past pastures dotted with tiny cows.

"Look at the baby cows!" Byron yells.

"I want to pet one!" Pippa cries.

"They are even trained to be on a harness," Rose chimes in.

"Those are the cutest things I have ever seen," I say, delighted upon the sight of them.

"Oh, Mummy! We have to get some, we have to!" Louis cries.

No comments from Layla.

She's either still smarting from my rebuke, or she's planning to turn one of those cows into cheeseburgers when we aren't looking.

I'll go with my first, and much less disturbing, theory.

"If Phillip is okay with us having mini cows, we're going to get some," Rose says. "But because they need to live in the country, we need to make sure it's okay with him."

Phillip.

I remember Phillip from my research on the Palmerstons. Lord Phillip Coventry, Viscount Brookstone, is Rose's younger brother, and the middle child of the Coventry family. Due to ancient laws, he will inherit all the estates when they pass from their parents and become the Earl of Castleton, even though Rose is the oldest daughter.

When I came across photos online of Phillip, I wasn't quite prepared for what I found. He's what I would call devastatingly handsome. He's tall, with golden blond hair and blue eyes. In the most recent images I've seen of him, his skin seems kissed by the sun, with that warm, bronze glow. He's twenty-five, and in all the media images posted of him, he looks serious. Whether it was attending a society wedding in a dashing morning suit or snapped coming out of a nightclub, his face is always fixed in that expression.

I wonder why that is.

"Phillip will say yes," Layla says, speaking at last. "He always does."

Rose laughs. "That is because he indulges you way too much, my sweet."

"What does indulges mean?" Layla asks.

"Phillip always gives you what you want and is very gener-ous," Rose says, laughing. "That is what indulges means."

Hmm. As long as he doesn't indulge Layla turning one of those cows into dinner, we'll get along just fine, I think.

We pull up to the farm, and all the children begin talking at once. Rose gets out first and opens the door to undo Byron's buckle and help him out of his booster seat. I help Pippa with hers, and as soon as I'm out, she scrambles out behind me. I turn and get Louis out while Layla climbs out the other side.

I stand on the gravel and breathe the air in deep. Lord, there is something magical about this green English countryside! The pastures are carpets of deep emerald, and the sky overhead is a brilliant blue, dotted by wisps of white clouds streaking across the sky. The temperature is in the seventies, mild and beautiful.

Something stirs within me. Yes, I have lived in Carlsbad, California, for almost my whole life.

The mountains, the palm trees, the warm sun, and ocean were all home.

But this ... this feels different.

As if this land was always meant to be my home.

"Oh, McKenna, look, look at the baby cows!" Byron cries in delight, interrupting my thoughts.

Which is good, because I was about to have to claim allergies to explain the tears in my eyes if I kept thinking about these feelings within me.

"Let's pet them!" Pippa cries, taking steps toward the fence.

I gently put my hand on her arm to stop her. "Hold on," I say, laughing. "We need to ask if we can pet them first."

She stares up at me, concern filtering across her tiny face. "Do they bite?"

I glance at Rose. I'm in foreign territory with livestock questions.

"I don't think so, but we never want to touch an animal without permission," she says, holding each of the boys by the hand.

"Come here, Layla," I say cheerfully. "You can take my other hand if you like."

Layla scowls. "No."

"No what?" I ask, smiling. "Now, you don't have to hold my hand. I know you're six and the big sister. But I just asked you if you would like something—there's a polite way to tell me no."

She huffs. I think I'm pushing all the wrong buttons in her, but ones I need to push for her to grow.

"No, thank you," she says, scuffing the gravel with the toe of her shoe.

"Thank you, Layla," I say.

Now I hear the sound of more gravel crunching under approaching footsteps. I turn and find a man approaching us. He's in his forties, I'd say, and flashes us all a welcoming smile.

"You must be the Palmerstons," he says as he nears us. "Welcome to Wee Moos Farm. I'm Robert."

"Hello, I'm Rose." She smiles brightly at him. "It's a pleasure to meet you."

They shake hands, and then she turns to me. "And this is McKenna."

He extends his hand to me. "Pleasure."

I shake it. "Nice to meet you," I say.

"And these are my children," Rose says. "My eldest is Layla. And this is Byron, Pippa, and Louis."

His eyes widen as he takes in the triplets. "My goodness, you all look so alike!"

"We're triplets," Pippa says proudly.

"We all came from Mummy's tummy at the same time," Louis adds.

"Triplets! I've never met triplets before," Robert says, studying them.

I glance at Layla, and a frown twists at her tiny mouth. My heart catches. She must see and hear this all the time—how special the triplets are—while she stands in the background, fading away.

I'm going to make her feel special for being Layla, I vow. *She's going to test me and not trust me and push all my buttons as I push hers, but I will make her feel wonderful about being Layla.*

Robert begins telling us about Wee Moos Farm and how he fell in love with miniature cattle. He's good at this, too. While he explains raising them to Rose, he also peppers his talk with tidbits aimed directly at the children to keep them engaged.

"They make wonderful pets," he says. "Just like a dog."

"So we can bring them home and keep them in the backyard?" Layla asks, intrigued by this idea.

"No, poppet, these mini cows will need to stay at Mooreton House," Rose explains.

"I raise some cattle to specifically be pets," Robert continues. "Before you take them, they are trained to be around people. They'll be able to walk on a leash by command."

"We can walk the cows?" Louis asks, his eyes wide.

"Yes, sir!" Robert says. "See those cows in front of you in the pasture? Those are miniature Herefords, and they can be walked on a leash."

"I want to try walking one!" Byron commands.

"Byron, we're still listening to Mr. Robert," I remind him.

"They do require hands-on time," Robert continues, turning to Rose. "Several times a week, they will need to get attention from you. Walking them, talking to them, petting them. This will keep them gentle and friendly."

Rose's brow furrows. I can tell she hadn't thought about that.

"Oh, dear," she says. "We live in London, and we only come out to the country for the weekends and for holiday. I wonder if our farm staff at Mooreton can handle this."

"You need to think about that," Robert advises. "You can leave them to their own devices and just have someone feed them and put them in the barn, that kind of thing, but there's no guarantee they'll stay docile."

I glance at Rose. Hadn't she done any homework on mini cows before coming out here? Or did she just see a picture of one on Pinterest and decide, "Those are cute! Let's have a herd!"

From the look on her face, I'm beginning to think it's the

latter.

"Mummy, can we see the cows now, please?" Pippa begs.

She blinks. "Oh, yes, let's do that!" she says brightly. "Robert, I saw you have the cute breed with the long hair, yes?"

He nods. "I do have the Scottish Highland. They are docile, but you do have to have the children mind the horns."

"Could they poke through someone?" Layla asks.

"They would hurt you, yes," Robert says.

Layla frowns.

"You simply have to learn to be careful of them," I say to Layla. "I know you could do it. And being the oldest, you can show your brothers and sisters how to be around them."

Her expression grows to one of surprise at my comment.

"I think they are so cute," Rose says.

Oh, she totally got this off a photo on Pinterest.

"What are these cows called?" Louis asks, pointing to the cows in front of us.

"Herefords," Robert says, smiling at them. "I have some right around the corner ready to meet you if you would like to see them."

All the children begin talking at once, and Robert leads us through a gate and into the pasture. The children are bursting over with excitement, and it brings a smile to my face.

And I get why they are excited. These mini cows are the cutest things I have ever seen in my life. There's a whole group of them happily grazing away under the English sun, with their white faces and reddish-brown coats.

"They need to be brushed and petted and even walked," Robert says as we approach. "Who can help with that?"

A chorus of "Me!" cries fill the air.

Robert laughs. "Good, I love having lots of helpers."

"Now, children, please be quiet and listen to what Mr. Robert tells us to do," I say.

They all fall silent. Even Layla looks very interested.

Robert walks them all over to a cow named Daisy. He shows us how to pet her and talk to her, and then hands a brush to Layla and gives her the task of brushing her. Soon, we all have brushes and are petting and stroking their coats, and it's magnificent. I've done petting zoos a million times with my previous nanny jobs, but nothing like this. Nothing compares to strolling around a rolling green pasture wearing Wellies and petting mini cows.

Robert puts harnesses on two mini cows and shows us how to walk them. I explain how we are all going to take turns, and first, I'm going to take Layla and Pippa out to walk Buttercup and Davey in the fields while Louis and Byron stay with their mother and give the other cows treats. Then I'll come back, and they'll walk the cows.

"I really get to do it first?" Layla asks, surprise in her tiny voice as Robert leaves us in the field with the two cows.

"Yes, of course, you do," I say, handing her the leash to Buttercup. "Now, Pippa, you're going to walk Davey. We're going to use some girl power and show the boys how to do this right."

"Girl power," Pippa giggles.

I grin at her. "We have lots of it locked inside of us. *Superpowers.*"

We begin walking the cows, and Layla and Pippa chatter happily in delight. I'm delighted myself. It's my first official day on the job, and I'm walking mini cows in the most beautiful countryside I have ever seen.

But as we're beginning to stroll along, I hear a shriek in the distance and more yelling. The cows grazing around us startle and begin to run. Pippa turns and lets go of her leash, and now Davey is running with his leash streaming behind him, and Buttercup struggles to get free.

I whip around, my nanny senses on red alert, and see Louis running wild, screaming, while Byron chases him with a look of fury on his face, something held up in his hand as he chases Louis.

It's *poo.*

"Girls, head back to your mum, we'll be back walking the cows in a minute!" I call out as I take off toward the boys.

"Boys! Stop running! Stop this very second!" I yell as I sprint the best I can in these rubber boots I have on. I also can't see, because my long, dark hair is now whipping around my face like a scarf and getting in my eyes. I quickly shove it aside, only to find they aren't listening to a word I say.

The mini cows have fled deep into the fields, and I have no idea how I'm going to retrieve Buttercup and Davey, but right now, my goal is to get Byron to drop that poo this very second.

"Byron!" I yell, gasping as I come closer, "Stop right now, you stop this instant!"

Louis sees me and runs toward me for protection. Byron holds the huge pile of poo like a baseball, ready to launch it at Louis.

"Byron! Dr—" but my command is cut off by another voice.

"*Byron!*" a voice bellows, breaking through the air like a crash of horrific thunder during a raging storm, "stop this instant!"

I turn toward the voice of doom, but as I do, I stumble in my new boots and go flailing. My arms shoot out, and I land with a huge thud onto the earth, my whole body slamming onto my back with force. I can't even cry out, as the wind is knocked straight out of me from the pain of the fall.

Good God, I think I see stars.

"McKenna!" Louis wails.

Now there's mooing and the sound of a herd running farther away and people running toward me. I'm still on my back, my head killing me, my back throbbing, and what is that mushy stuff underneath my head? Oh, no, I hope that's not blood!

"She's *dead!*" Louis cries hysterically. "Byron killed the nanny!"

I groan. I'm about to reply that I'm not dead when that voice returns.

"Back up!" the same deep voice I heard earlier commands with powerful authority. Suddenly, the sun I felt a second earlier on my face is blocked. "Miss? Miss? Can you hear me?"

I open my eyes.

And towering over me is Phillip Coventry, Viscount Brookstone.

Chapter Two

I gaze up at Phillip, the sun shining around his head like a fuzzy halo. I feel as if the wind has been knocked out of me twice now. Once by my fall, the second time by staring up at the gorgeous face of this man standing over me.

He's a *Greek god*, so beautiful and perfect that he must have been dropped from the heavens above and straight into this cow pasture to help me.

Social media images don't do Phillip Coventry justice. He's tall and broad—I can see that from the fabric of the blue button-down shirt that is stretching across his shoulders. He drops down next to me, gently placing a hand on my arm as he stares down into my eyes.

"McKenna, how is your head?" he asks, his eyes flickering over me in concern. "Can you speak to me?"

A frisson runs through me as his deep voice fills the space between us. Lord, his eyes are so *blue*. A million clichés about blue eyes fill my mind, but none suit him, as they are such a beautiful, vivid color. His hair is thick and blond, with the sun dancing across his waves and giving them a rich, golden glow.

"Bloody hell, is she knocked out?" I hear Rose yelling, and the sound of her breathing heavily as if she's sprinted across the pasture. "Do we need to call an ambulance?"

"I didn't kill her!" Byron cries hysterically. "She fell on her own!"

"You made her run, and now the nanny is dead!" Louis screams back.

"This is so much worse than turning the mini cows into mini burgers!" Layla cries in triumph. "You both killed the nanny! Now you'll go to *jail!*"

"Nobody is going to jail," Phillip says. "McKenna, please, can you say anything? Tell me where you have pain?"

"I ..." Damn, my head really hurts. Oh, wait, blood! I shake my head. "Am I bleeding? At the back of my head?"

"Mummy!" Louis calls out. "She's not dead!"

"Boys, back up," Phillip commands. He gently brushes some of my hair aside, checking for what I fear will be a pool of blood from a cut. "No, I don't see blood. Can I help you sit up? Do you think you can do that?"

Soon, Rose is standing over me, and her hand flies to her mouth. "Oh, God, McKenna, I'm so sorry! We need to get you to the hospital!"

"No," I say firmly. "I don't think I have a concussion. Just bumped the back of my head."

"Here, I'll help you up," Phillip says, sliding one of his hands underneath my shoulder blade. His hand is large and warm—I can feel his heat through the thin fabric of my shirt.

I push myself upright, and Phillip's hand remains on my back as I sit up, supporting me. *Ouch.* Pain shoots through me, and everything smarts. My head, my back, and my tailbone. But then I feel something sliding down my neck. And what's that smell? It smells lik—

Plop! As soon as it hits the ground, the lovely aroma of cow manure fills the air. And the scent is wafting up from … *me.*

No. It can't be what I think it is, can it?

"It smells over here!" Pippa says, pinching her nose closed. "Ew, I'm going to be sick!"

I turn to Phillip. "It's not blood oozing from the back of my head, is it?" I ask, cringing.

His gaze shifts to the ground behind me, then he lifts his blue eyes back to meet mine. "Um, no."

Oh, God. *I'm* the one who smells, and it's because I've landed in a pile of cow shit.

"Mummy, I don't feel well," Pippa says.

I glance at her. Oh, no, the child looks green.

"Pip—" I begin.

Splat! Too late. Pippa has now tossed her lunch a few feet from me in the field.

She bursts into tears.

"Oh, no, I'm so sorry!" Rose cries. She scoops up Pippa in her arms, and Pippa wraps her tiny arms around Rose's neck. "We'll leave right now. I don't know what got into Byron. He thought Louis was taking the cow he wanted to brush, and then … well, you know. Little boys will be little boys, right?"

"She's in no shape to watch the children now," Phillip says, his tone firm and commanding. "Rose, go get them together where you can manage them. I'll help McKenna."

"Buttercup and Davey," I say.

"Who?" Phillip asks, his golden brows forming into a V of confusion on his face.

"Mini cows. They ran off into the pasture. They have leashes on."

"I'll let Robert know, he can retrieve them," Rose says. Then she turns to her boys. "Mummy is very upset over what has happened today. We might not be getting mini cows now."

That announcement results in screaming and protests, and the nanny in me, despite my pounding head, can't take it.

"Boys!" I say sharply, so much so that they both whip around and stare at me. "This is no way to behave. I'm so disappointed our fun adventure has ended this way. Seeing the mini cows is a treat. When you act poorly, the treats are taken away. And that makes me so sad. I think it makes you sad, too."

Louis stares at me with saucer eyes. Byron's lower lip comes out.

"Please mind your mummy now," I say gently. "I have a bit of a headache. But I think you owe Mr. Robert an apology for acting so badly on his farm and scaring the cows away. When I'm better, we'll talk about this. But I do know in my heart that you can behave better."

They stare at me in surprise. I wait for Louis to say he didn't try to kill me and for Byron to claim that he was wronged by Louis.

"But we didn't do anything, we should still have cows," Pippa says, gesturing between herself and Layla.

"Yes, we should have our cows and the boys none," Layla declares. "And if I want to turn mine into burgers, I can!"

Louis shrieks. "McKenna said you wouldn't eat them!"

"Stop it," Phillip commands. His voice once again rolls like thunder across the pasture, and I don't even think the cows dare move at this point. "Your nanny is *hurt*. You need to be thinking about *her*. McKenna needs you all to behave and be quiet until she can get up, do you understand me?"

You need to be thinking about her. My God, he is descended from above.

All of the children, and Rose, stare back at Phillip with large

18

eyes. Wow. It's crystal clear that while Rose might be older and their mother, Viscount Brookstone has their respect.

"Not a word, or I will be very disappointed that you are not minding your nanny," Phillip continues.

Nobody protests.

"Well, right, I'll go watch the children while you recover," Rose says. "Come along, children."

Now everyone is walking away, and I'm sitting with Phillip in the middle of a pasture.

"Are you sure you don't need a doctor?" he asks, his voice full of concern.

I turn my attention toward him, butterflies shifting in my stomach. "No, I'm going to be sore, and I stink, but I'll be okay. Thank you, um, Your Grace? I'm sorry, I don't know if you are Your Grace or Your Lord or Viscount Brookstone or Lord Coventry or Mr. Coventry."

His eyes stay locked on mine. "None of the above."

I blink. "None?"

"Phillip. Just Phillip."

I smile. "Oh. Now, that I can do."

"I guessed as much," he quips. "Let me know when you're ready to stand up."

As the scent of cow manure and Pippa's puke waft toward me, I decide I'm more than ready to stand up and at least step a few feet away before I end up like poor Pippa.

"I'm ready," I say.

Phillip rises and sticks his hand out to me. I suck in a breath as I put my hand in his. Oh my, his hand is massive, and mine is so small in his! He clasps it with a firm grip and helps me up, and just like that, I'm standing mere inches from him.

Now I'm aware of the span of his chest, and how his slim-fit shirt hugs his frame, tapering to his waist.

A new scent fills the air, one besides cow manure and English grass and country air.

It's the scent of him.

His skin smells of vanilla and spice and leather, a scent that is both warm and sweet, and utterly lavish.

And completely captivating.

I blush as he releases my hand. "Thank you."

"You had quite a fall," Phillip says. "Is your vision okay?"

Oh, that it is, I think as I stare up at him.

I nod. "Fine."

"Dizziness?"

"No."

"Headache?"

I shake my head. "My head smarts, but no major headache."

"Look me in the eyes," Phillip says.

I laugh. "I'm not lying to you."

For the first time, I see the corners of his mouth curve up, as if he wants to smile.

"No, not that, just look at me."

Mystified, I stare into his eyes.

"Your pupils look fine. That's another thing to check. You don't seem confused, either."

"No, I'm not. Except for the fact that you are here. Rose didn't say you were meeting us."

He cocks an eyebrow. "Rose didn't know. She told me she was coming here to take the children here to see mini cows. I casually asked when she was doing that and made a plan to surprise her here. Otherwise, she would have bought a herd of them on impulse and them dropped them on my doorstep to figure out."

I smile. I don't say anything against my new employer, but I have a feeling this could have easily happened today.

"But back to your fall. You should be on alert for all of those things," he says. "Confusion, fuzziness, sensitivity to light, mental fog."

"You know a lot of those symptoms," I tease.

"I had a concussion after a fall from a horse," Phillip says. "I had some of those symptoms."

I nod. I want to ask him about his fall, but I don't know if I'm allowed to talk to him. I mean, he's Rose's *brother*. I'm sure he doesn't really care to talk to the nanny. He's being kind to make sure I'm okay, but I doubt he's here to spend his afternoon talking to me.

"Are you okay to go on back?" Phillip asks.

"Yes, of course. Feel free to walk ahead of me. I know I smell horrid."

Now I see it. A bit of a smile plays at his mouth. And I must have hit my head hard, because my heart skips happily upon sight of it.

"Whilst you do have, uh, a remarkable scent about you," he says slowly, "I don't mind."

I burst out laughing, and he looks at me in surprise.

"Oh, that is the nicest way anyone could ever say I smell like sh—" I stop myself from swearing in front of him.

"You can swear in front of me, the children can't hear," he says, dropping his voice as if we are conspiring together.

We begin walking across the lush green grass, our Wellingtons nearly stepping in unison as we move next to each other.

"Okay, you are so polite, you found a way to nicely say I smell like shit," I say, grinning. "Now that tells me you have a gift with words."

"You think so?" he asks, sounding surprised.

"If you can make me feel like I smell remarkable with cow poo stuck in my hair, you indeed have a gift."

Once again, I'm rewarded with a hint of a smile. "I'll take that as a compliment."

"Oh, it is," I insist.

"In the spirit of candor, I detect something else in the air."

"Oh, don't tell me I picked up Pippa's vomit on my clothing," I groan. I do a quick check by trying to look at the back of my shirt, and then the back of my sleeves, praying I don't see anything else disgusting splattered across me.

"Good God, no, that I'd have to find a word beyond remarkable for," Phillip says.

I quit looking for puke and glance back at him. His are locked in on my face. My heart skips a beat once again.

"What else do you detect?" I ask.

"Coffee and vanilla," he says. "Is that your perfume?"

"Yes," I say, alarmed at how my heart has suddenly gone from skipping to running as I stare up at Phillip. "It's Yves Saint Laurent Black Opium. Which has coffee and vanilla notes. Well, according to the salesperson who helped me, it does. She said it had black coffee and vanilla notes."

"She would be correct," Phillip says. "It's ... lovely on you."

Ooh!

Phillip clears his throat and shifts his gaze straight ahead, so I do the same, with my heart going crazy in the process. Which is stupid, because he is my employer's brother. I need to remember this moment for what it is. A moment when a sexy viscount told me he liked my perfume and nothing more.

"Thank you," I say, keeping my gaze straight ahead, as I don't dare look at him for fear of more butterflies taking off in my stomach.

We walk along in silence for a few moments. I see Rose is still holding Pippa, Layla has busied herself brushing a cow, and the boys are standing next to her, no doubt a form of time out.

"I think we're ready to go," Rose says. "Layla, love, say goodbye to the cow and come along now."

"Mummy, I can't be next to McKenna, she smells really bad," Pippa says. "Like really, really stinky bad!"

Crap. She's right. Even though I can change my clothes, thanks to my suitcase in the trunk, it's in my freaking hair. I need a long scrubbing in a shower before I smell normal again.

"I smell it, too, McKenna smells bad," Byron says. "I don't want to sit by her."

"I'll be sick again" Pippa insists.

"Me, too!" Byron claims. "My stomach is starting to hurt!"

Die. I want to die. I'm the stinky nanny nobody can bear to ride with for God knows how long until we reach their country home in Northamptonshire because my scent is revolting.

"McKenna, you can change your clothing. You can get some out of your suitcase," Rose says.

"Yes, I will, but my hair," I say, gesturing to my head. "It's in my hair."

"Oh," Rose says, blinking, as she hadn't thought of that.

A wind comes up and blows across us, and good God, I can't even stand the scent of me. Rose must smell the manure, because she blinks several times as she tries not to wrinkle her nose but fails and screws it up the tiniest bit as she detects my foul aroma.

Layla returns to us, and Rose directs her to a hand sanitization station outside the gate. "Wash your hands, Layla."

"P.U.," Layla declares as she sticks her hands under the faucet.

"That smells *bad*."

"All right, enough. McKenna, why don't you get a change of clothes from your bag?" Phillip says. "Rose, after she does, take the kids and go. She can't travel in the same car as the kids. And I think after hitting her head, she could do with some peace and quiet."

"But who will take her back to Mooreton House?" Rose asks.

"I will," Phillip says, much to my shock. "She can come with me."

Chapter Three

"Are you sure you don't want to call a car to come get me?" I ask, hesitating before I open the door to Phillip's silver Jaguar coupe. "You have a beautiful car, and I am essentially going to put a pasture in it."

Phillip puts a trash bag filled with my clothing in the trunk and slams it shut. He looks at me. "I could, but they don't exactly have Ubers roaming around the English countryside looking for passengers."

I blush. Of course not.

"But," Phillip says, walking around to his side of the car, "even if this had happened in London, I'd still drive you home. I'm not worried about the car. I'm more worried about you. How are you feeling?"

My breath catches. He's a proper gentleman. Phillip is considerate and kind, even though I'm the hired help for his sister—he doesn't have to care at all about me, but he does.

"Like I need twenty shampoos, but other than that, fine," I say, smiling at him.

His mouth curves up again in that faint smile. "Come on, let's go."

I slide into the sleek sports car and sit on a blanket Phillip has spread out on the seat for me. He slips behind the wheel, and his massive frame fills the small space. I notice how his thighs are huge in his jeans. And I'm acutely aware of how his sensual cologne is mixing with the leather scent of the car seats.

I turn and look out the window as Phillip starts the Jaguar. Loud music fills the car, and he quickly turns it down. I recognize it, though. I glance at his console, and indeed, it was "Persona Non Grata" by Bright Eyes.

"Do you like indie folk music?" I ask.

"I do," he says, turning the car around on the gravel path. "I get tired of the house music I always hear at the clubs."

I study him. *He doesn't seem like the club type,* I muse, studying his profile. But then again, I really don't know him. Yet in all of the pictures of him leaving exclusive clubs around London, Phillip has never looked happy.

But to be fair, I wouldn't look happy at two o'clock in the morning with photographers in my face, either.

I look out the window again. I don't want to bother him, since it's not as if his plans today included driving his sister's nanny around.

"Um, do you mind if I crack the windows a bit?" Phillip asks.

I blush furiously. "Oh, no, I'm so sorry."

"No, nothing a bit of fresh air can't fix. Or help," he says, glancing at me.

And then I see it.

That whisper of a smile. Even though I would love to see a full smile, knowing I can see a hint of what it could be sets my heart fluttering.

"Of course, please, crack the windows," I say.

Phillip lowers both windows a bit, and soon we are off, driving down beautiful English country roads as we head toward

Mooreton House.

"What made you come to England?" Phillip suddenly asks, breaking the silence.

Startled, I turn to him. "Pardon?" I ask, surprised that he wants to engage in conversation.

"I'm sorry, was that too personal of a question? You don't have to answer."

"No, I don't mind," I say. I clear my throat. "I came to find myself. You see, my mother was British. I was born here."

"Really?" Phillip asks, and I can hear the surprise in his voice.

"Yes. My mother and father lived in Essex when I was an infant. But when I was six months old, my mother was killed in a car accident. With her parents."

A breath of air escapes Phillip's lips. "My God, I'm so sorry."

For some reason I can't explain, I feel the need to share details. Details I rarely talk about.

"It was my mother's birthday," I say, my voice quiet even to my own ears. "I had been fussy all day with teething, and Dad came home from work and saw my mum truly needed to get out and have a nice dinner. A break. So, he offered to stay home with me instead. My grandparents picked up Mum to take her to the restaurant, but they never made it. My grandfather had a heart attack while driving and crashed the car into a telephone pole. They all died instantly."

"Oh, my God," Phillip whispers. "McKenna, I'm so sorry."

"I obviously don't remember her," I admit, and to my surprise, a lump appears in my throat. "My dad was devastated by her death, and he took me back to California, where he was from, so his family could help him raise me. His dream had been to live in London with Mum someday, but those dreams died with the accident. With her."

"I can't imagine the pain he must have been in," Phillip says, his brow furrowing as he thinks of it. "And having to raise an infant without the woman he loved."

"He never speaks of the accident, or her, other than to explain what happened when I was old enough to understand it," I say. "He remarried when I was four. And my mom—and she really is my mom—loved me as if I were her own. So, I was very lucky to have a true family. But when Dad remarried, contact with my British side of the family eventually fell off. I know they didn't want to interfere, but I feel like now, as an adult, I want to know them. I want to know things about my mum. I want ... I want to find a part of myself that's missing."

Tears prick my eyes, and I quickly look down at my hands, which are folded in my lap, and try to blink the tears away.

"I'm so sorry for everything you have been through," he says. "That's a heavy past to sort through."

I nod. "Sometimes ... no, never mind."

"What?" Phillip asks.

I swallow. It's something I've never said aloud to anyone, even my closest friends, so why would I say it to Phillip? I glance at his profile. I don't know him, yet I want to confide in him. Is that crazy? Is my head messed up from that fall? Or is it because he's shown such compassion for someone he barely knows that I think he might understand?

"I feel like the accident was my fault," I say, the words coming out in a whisper.

"Oh, McKenna, no," Phillip says, shaking his head. "You can't think that way."

I swallow hard before speaking. "If I hadn't been fussy, we would have gone out as a family. We ... we would have met my grandparents at the restaurant. She would have lived."

"I know I'm speaking out of turn, but I'm going to say something I think you need to hear," Phillip says. "You are not responsible for this. If you've been carrying that weight around on your shoulders, you need to let it go. Terrible things happen to good people, for no reason at all. It's horrible and painful, but it's also life."

"I know you're right, but I can't help but wonder if things would have been different if I hadn't been fussy. If I hadn't been such a burden on her all day long, so she needed a break," I say, and my voice breaks off as, oh, no, I feel like I'm going to cry. I turn and watch the countryside roll by, trying to find something to fixate on so I don't break down in front of Phillip.

To my shock, I feel Phillip's hand. I glance down, and I'm not dreaming. His large hand is over mine in a comforting, reassuring gesture.

"McKenna. Something could have happened to your mum the next day. The next week. We'll never know. Our time here on this earth is limited, and hers was tragically short. But it's not your cross to bear. It's not—and *never* has been—your fault."

I bite down hard on my lower lip, trying to keep back the ugly cry that is threatening to break forth from my chest. He squeezes my hands with his, his huge fingers wrapping both my hands in his, and I can't help it. A sob escapes my throat. I wait for him to jerk his hand back, but he doesn't.

"I-I'm going t-to ugly cry!" I spit out.

"What?" Phillip asks, his brows drawing into a confused V.

I burst into tears, sobbing loudly. Tears are streaming, my nose is starting to run, and never have I hated being an ugly crier more than I have in this moment.

"Christ!" Phillip says, his eyes large in shock.

I want to tell him that I rarely cry, but when I do, it's messy and nothing to be alarmed about, but of course, I'm now in a fit of ugly crying and can't tell him that because my chest is heaving, and the sobs are loud and painful sounding, and I can't get enough air to speak.

Phillip removes his hand, and oh, no, I've gone a bridge too far with him. Now he's stuck with the crazy, ugly-crying nanny, and he doesn't want to deal with me.

Suddenly, he whips the car onto the side of the road, as if he needs to pull over for a mechanical issue. Or to throw a hysterical nanny out, take your pick. He shuts off the engine, and I wait for him to ask what the hell is wrong with me, but before I can, he leaps out of the car.

Shit! He's so over my hysterics, he has to get away from me. Gah, I'm going to be fired. On day one. Phillip is going to tell Rose I'm an emotional lunatic who should be kept far away from the children.

Before I can cry about this, the passenger door is jerked open. I jump back in my seat, startled.

"McKenna, get out of the car," Phillip says.

Oh, my God, is he going to abandon me on the side of the road? He's going to throw me and my trash bag of shitty clothing out and leave me here, isn't he?

I undo the seatbelt and get out of the car. We're next to rolling fields of green, and the sun is shining brightly, and normally, I'd want my camera to capture this magical beauty around me, but instead, I'm bawling and quite possibly about to be ditched in the middle of nowhere, so I have bigger concerns than capturing the countryside to remember forever.

I step out of the car, and as soon as I do, I find myself in Phillip's arms. He's drawn me into his chest, one hand spanning my back, the other holding the back of my head. I stop sobbing.

30

I can't breathe. My cheek is pressed to his chest, and I can feel the soft fabric of his shirt and hear the beating of his heart.

"It's okay," he murmurs, his voice reverberating through every inch of me. "Let it go. Right here, let it go."

My heart thunders in my ears. I can't process all the things that are happening. Phillip didn't pull the car over in disgust. He stopped the car to hold me. To comfort me, to encourage me to get these feelings of a horrific past out of my heart and head.

And now I'm in his arms.

My tears subside as shock takes over. Phillip is holding me. He's rubbing my back. He has his hand in my hot mess hair, not caring if he touches manure. Phillip isn't telling me to stop crying or being hysterical or to take a breath.

He is telling me to cry.

Phillip wants me to be me.

I instinctively move my arms around his back and allow myself to weep. I've kept so much of this inside for so many years. I didn't want to hurt my mom or dad. I didn't dare bring up a past that caused so much pain. But now, with Phillip? He's given me permission to do just that. As I stand on the side of the road, in the country that gave me my mother, in a country that is a part of me, in the arms of a viscount, I allow myself to unburden all the guilt I have shoved down in my heart for my entire life.

Finally, after I've cried all the tears until I have none left, I grow quiet. Phillip still hasn't said a word. I take a step back from him, and with horror, I see I have cried and snotted all over his shirt.

"Oh, my God," I gasp. "Your shirt! I-I think that could be snot!"

Phillip glances down and then back up at me. "So?"

"So? *So?* I just met you, and I've gotten snot all over your shirt! And I'm sure you have manure on your hands from touching my hair, and I've *ugly cried* in front of you. I've clung on to you and touched you, and this is about the worst first impression anyone could ever make on another human being!" I cry.

Phillip's eyes meet mine. "No. It's about the most real introduction I've ever had to another human being."

I shake my head, as the gravity of what I have done sinks in now that I've stopped crying. "This is so inappropriate. I'm the help."

His eyes flash. "Did I hire you?"

I stare up into his eyes. "Well, no."

"Did I put my hand on yours first?"

"Well, yes."

"Did I pull you into my arms, or did you fling yourself into them?"

"You embraced me," I answer.

"You are not my employee, so stop saying that," Phillip says firmly. "I don't want you to apologize for any of this. So many things in my life are planned and manipulated, and this was a choice, to be with you. Don't take one of my few choices away from me."

I stare up at him, confused by his confession to me. What does that mean, few choices? But before I can question it, Phillip lets go of my arms and takes a step back from me.

"Sorry," he says, shaking his head.

"Don't say you're sorry for being real right back to me," I say gently.

Something shifts in his blue eyes, as if he's going to guard whatever he just said to me very closely.

"I have wipes in the boot," he says. "Let me get them."

I stand still as Phillip moves back around to the driver's side and opens the door. He pops the trunk and goes to the back of the car, retrieving a packet of wipes.

I decide to change the subject, as I can tell Phillip doesn't want to talk about himself.

"I'm impressed you have those," I call out to him.

A hint of a smile returns to his face. "You've met my nieces and nephews. I can't go anywhere without these. They're always muddy, sticky, or snotty. Or is that you I'm talking about?"

Then I see it. A huge smile lights up his face, and oh, my God, it's the most beautiful smile I have ever seen. His eyes are shining brightly, and his smile is warm and inviting, as if I could talk to him for hours and he'd grant me more of them.

And it's genuine, I think as I stare at him.

Now all I want to do is make Phillip happy enough to keep that smile on his face.

"I wouldn't be a good nanny if I weren't all those things on a daily basis," I say, smiling back at him.

He wipes his hands and puts that wipe aside. Then he takes another one and dabs at the front of his shirt, which makes me blush with embarrassment.

"My God, you did blow your nose on my shirt," he quips.

"I did not!" I protest, cringing. "You make it sound like I used it like a tissue."

"Well?" he says, gesturing to the front of his shirt. "Didn't you?"

Then he grins again, but this time, it's a wicked smile.

Now my heart is pounding and I feel butterflies, and it's so wrong. I can't be attracted to Phillip. He's my employer's brother—this is on the first page of Nanny 101 for things not to do when you are a nanny.

Besides, I don't want to form feelings for anyone. I don't need to be hurt, and this has hurt written all over it. My boss's brother. A viscount. This will not end well for me on any level, if anything were to ever happen.

And that's a big if.

Like put an asterisk beside it, bold it, underline it, and italicize it *if.*

Regardless of what Phillip is thinking, I do know I have always fiercely protected my heart, never allowing any man to get too close.

Yet Phillip, within an hour of meeting him, has gotten closer than any previous boyfriend ever has.

He shuts the trunk and turns to me. "Are you okay now?"

No, I think, my mind reeling. *I'm not. You're turning everything upside down, and I barely know you.*

While there is panic, I also have a strange sense of … what's the word I'm looking for?

Right.

That being in England is right. Standing on this soil, working in the country my mum loved so much, and breathing this air is right.

The same kind of right that I felt when Phillip drew me into his arms.

It's *right.*

I swallow hard. I have no idea how I'm going to reconcile these feelings.

"McKenna, are you okay?" Phillip repeats.

I decide to answer from my heart.

"Yes," I say softly.

For the first time in my life, I don't feel the accident was my fault. The past has been lifted from me, thanks to Phillip.

And as I gaze at him, I wonder if he can free me from more than that if I'm brave enough to let him in.

Chapter Four

I feel like a whole new woman on Saturday morning. Well, I'm battered and sore, but still. I feel like myself again.

Of course, I already felt a million times better after taking an indulgently long, hot shower and washing my hair five times as soon as I arrived at Mooreton House. Once the children were put down for bed, I had the rest of the evening to unpack and relax. I was given a large room for the weekend.

And not just large, but incredible.

I walk across the antique floral rug on the floor and allow my eyes to drink it in for the millionth time in wonder. This room is appointed with a massive, four-poster canopy bed, a chaise lounge that is perfect for reading, and a beautiful antique desk for writing letters. If I had the need to write a letter, I could sit down right now and pen one, it's so inviting. It's quiet and peaceful up here, and the morning sun is streaming through the huge windows that overlook the lush grounds below.

I move to the window and part the curtain a bit so I can peer outside at the massive topiary gardens below. My God, to think the Coventry family calls this place a country house.

It's the biggest estate I've ever seen in my life.

The Mooreton House website didn't do it justice. When Phillip drove up the long drive leading to a looming house in the distance, I couldn't believe what I was seeing. I already knew the house was built in 1600 and has 102 rooms, set upon eleven thousand acres of lush English countryside. The property has forests, manicured gardens, and fields of grazing sheep. But seeing it in person? My God. I find it hard to believe people still live here. While it is a tourist attraction and the state rooms are open to visitors, this is still considered a family home.

A home that has belonged to the Coventry family for more than *four hundred years.* This is all they've ever known. This is the life they live, in this massive estate and in the posh, historic townhome in London.

And all of this will belong to Phillip one day.

Phillip.

I catch a glimpse of myself in the window, and I'm smiling as soon as he enters my mind. Even in my reflection, I can see my brown eyes are full of sparkle and light. My smile is wide, and the dimple is visible in my left cheek. I can see the glow in my expression, all generated by mere thoughts of Phillip Coventry.

I sigh happily with memories of yesterday. We conversed the whole drive from the farm to Mooreton House. I learned that he studied land economy at Cambridge, to prepare him for running the family estate in the future. Right now, he told me, he's working on developing revenue streams to keep the family estate growing, but then he fell strangely silent, as if the subject had opened up all kinds of doors in his head—doors he preferred to remain locked and closed. I didn't feel right pressing him on it, and when he quickly changed the subject back to me, I let him.

He asked me questions about California, as he has never been there, and if I had seen all the touristy things in the state, like the Golden Gate Bridge and the Hollywood Walk of Fame. I told him everything he wanted to know about my home state, and then he asked how I came to work with children. I eagerly shared how I've always loved being around them, because they are so bright and open to the world. I even told him that my big dream is to design educational programs and curriculum for organizations and schools to nurture and grow children's inquisitive natures and inspire confidence.

For someone who seemed so serious, Phillip talked easily to me as he drove, about likes and dislikes and how different our life experiences had been so far. When we arrived at Mooreton House, however, he disappeared. After I showered and changed, I came down and tended to the children. I was surprised to learn there was no chef and Rose would be doing the cooking. It must have shown on my face, because she explained that Phillip struck the chef from the budget, and it was a stupid decision if you asked her, because she can't cook. I had to hide a smile at that, as in the car, Phillip confided that his father let his sisters run amok with finances, and when he took them over last year, they were both cross with him for a long time.

So, with Rose in charge of dinner, she served the children frozen fish fingers and chips. Then she invited me to dinner with herself and John, where we had ... frozen fish fingers and chips.

Maybe that's why Phillip didn't come down for dinner. He knew what was going to be served.

But when he didn't come down like I had hoped he would, I was reminded of the truth. Phillip Coventry is kind to me, but that's probably where this all ends. He could have been out with friends or on a date, for all I know. Or merely preferred to stay holed up in a different wing of the house for a whole evening.

Regardless, while I found myself eager to spend more time with him, he did not feel the same. Kindness for an emotional mess of a nanny is one thing. Killing time during a long drive with pleasant conversation falls in the same category.

None of that means Phillip likes me, even as a friend.

Considering the rather large fact that I'm working for his sister, this is for the best. I can admire Phillip from afar and keep my job safely intact.

As well as my heart.

My heart? I gasp in horror at the thought that popped into my head. Where did that come from? I have never had to worry about my heart before. I've had boyfriends, but whenever they showed signs of falling in love, I ended it. I couldn't stay with someone when I didn't reciprocate the feelings. So my heart has never gone down that path—I've never felt anything more than caring about someone.

So why did I think of protecting it just now?

An unsettling feeling sweeps over me, one I don't like, and one I can't name. I firmly shove all of this stupidness out of my head. It's time to start the day. It's right before six o'clock, as I want to get up, eat, and have a cup of coffee before the kids are awake.

I leave my room and move through the large corridor, study-ing all the portraits of relatives staring back at me from the walls. Okay, this is kind of creepy. My parents have modern art back in Carlsbad. I'm not used to having eyes follow me as I walk.

But one painting in particular makes me pause. There's a full-sized portrait at the end of the hall. I pass the staircase, which I was going to take to head downstairs, and go straight to the artwork that has captured my eye. I stop a few feet from it, and normally, I'd marvel at how it is life-sized, with a man well over six feet tall captured in the picture.

But that's not what drew me to the portrait.

The man looks like Phillip.

I stare at the oil painting in amazement. The man is young, in his twenties, with the same golden curls and piercing blue eyes that Phillip has. The same nose, even. My God. It's insane how much this man looks like Phillip!

He's dressed in a white muslin shirt with a vest over it and fawn-colored pants. A large overcoat in dark brown is over the top, and a white type of scarf is tied at his neck. He has a cane in his right hand and his left hand on his hip, looking posh and distinguished in this pose.

But the expression is what I can't get over. It's identical to Phillip's. There's no hint of a smile, no light in his eyes, just a quiet seriousness to him.

Yet yesterday, once Phillip pulled over on the side of the road, this version disappeared. There was light and empathy in his eyes. Smiles that started slowly with just a curve at the corners of his mouth but then became full ones the longer I was in his presence.

"Do you feel like you've seen this man before?" a low, deep voice asks from behind.

I jump five feet in the air, and a strangled scream escapes my lips. My heart is beating out of my chest as I whirl around to find Phillip standing behind me.

"Oh, my God," I say, my hand flying over my heart. "I didn't mean to scream, but you scared me to death!"

He smiles, that same smile that I saw yesterday, and I feel warmth spread through my body as a result.

"I'm sorry," he says. "But if it makes you feel better, you

didn't wake anyone up. One, Rose and John are down another corridor. Two, those kids sleep like the dead unless it's Christmas morning. Then they are up at four a.m. demanding we all get up."

"Oh," I say, relieved.

Phillip walks toward me. Today, he's dressed in jeans and a white button-down shirt that is untucked and has the sleeves rolled up. A rugged, silver watch adorns his left wrist, and a pair of cool, suede desert boots are the perfect accessory for dressing down.

He moves beside me, and immediately, his presence fills the space at the end of this corridor. Everything about Phillip takes up room, from his sheer size to the deep voice that resonates to the cologne that is lingering on his skin.

"How are you feeling? Any headaches or other symptoms?" he asks.

My heart warms from his concern. "I'm fine. Truly fine. Thank you for asking.'

"I'm glad to hear that," he says. "I was worried."

Ooh!

His eyes linger on my face, and I find my heart thumping a little faster inside my chest. Then he quickly clears his throat and shifts his gaze to the picture in front of us. "So, I see you've met the other Phillip," he says.

I feel my own eyes widen in surprise. "His name is actually Phillip?"

He nods. "Yes. This is Phillip, the Earl of Castleton. His father was a big gambler who ran up some huge debts in his time. Property had to be sold off to pay them, and the only things remaining are this house and the one in London. His father died young—killed in a duel, of all things—and Phillip inherited the

41

mess when he was eighteen. He had to make drastic decisions to keep the estates afloat and sold off family heirlooms to do it. But he managed to save what he could, and that is what we have today."

"A duel?" I ask, incredulous. "You actually have a relative who died in a *duel?*"

"Indeed," Phillip says.

"You look so much like him. You don't duel, do you?" I joke.

An amused smile plays at the corners of his mouth. "I haven't had a reason to pull out my pistols lately."

I study the portrait. "You look so much like him. Down to the serious expression on the mouth."

"What? I don't have that."

"Are you joking?" I ask, laughing. "Of course, you do! See the way his corners turn down?" I point to that part of the oil painting. "You have that exact same expression."

"I don't look *this* serious," Phillip protests.

I glance up at him. He's staring at the picture as if he's never seen it before. Like he's sorting out a puzzle.

Phillip honestly has no idea how serious he appears all the time, I think with amazement.

"You're wrong. I definitely do not look this ... this ..." He frowns, and I know he can't come up with a suitable word replacement for serious.

"Sour?" I suggest.

"*Sour?*" he asks. "You think I look *sour?*"

"Is grim a better choice?" I provide helpfully, grinning gleefully at him.

"Oh, you are so getting in trouble," Phillip says.

And my heart leaps when I see the wicked gleam in his eyes.

"Grave," I continue. "Oh, wait, what about humorless?"

"That's it. I'm telling Rose to hire a nanny from one of those posh nanny schools who will respect me as the viscount and sack you instead."

I laugh loudly at that empty threat. Then, to my surprise, he chuckles. The sound reverberates through me, practically creating a hum through my body. I've never heard him laugh before, and while this isn't a full one, the sound of joy coming from him causes butterflies in my stomach.

"Well, I don't know if you can handle it," Phillip says, "seeing as I'm grim and all, but would you like to come downstairs and have breakfast? I typically make a full English on the weekend."

My pulse quickens. I know it shouldn't. I know this means nothing, and I should say no, but the idea of spending time with Phillip is too good to pass up.

"Unless you are a typical California girl who likes juice or avocado toast," Phillip teases.

"I'm going to tell you right now, I'm not a typical California girl. And I'm half-British, remember?"

"Oh, right. So, you'd be game for black pudding and beans on toast this morning?" Phillip asks, quirking a brow up. "Your British side would *love* that."

I make a face, trying to picture what on earth he's talking about. "That sounds disgusting."

"I'll take that as a no," he says. "Come on, let's walk and talk."

I move beside Phillip as we begin to walk toward the large, sweeping staircase.

"If you were in Carlsbad, what would you make yourself for breakfast?" he asks.

"An acai bowl," I say. "I'm obsessed with those."

"Right. Your traditional British side is definitely showing

with that choice."

I laugh. "Oh, shut up," I say without even thinking.

Then it happens.

He laughs.

A rich, down from the bottom of his gut, full on, brilliant laugh.

I nearly trip over the steps, I'm so shocked by the beautiful sound of it.

"I believe that should be 'Shut up, *my lord,'*" he declares.

"My lord? Oh, no, we're not going down that path," I tease back.

"I believe we are going down the stairs," he quips.

I groan. "I would retort, but then you'd probably demand I call you my lord, Viscount Brookstone, Your Grace, or some other ridiculously long title."

"You can call me anything you want. It doesn't mean there will be an acai bowl in it for you."

I laugh. I love this funny interior that is buried beneath his serious exterior.

"What else do you eat for breakfast back home?" Phillip asks.

"Chia pudding."

"Good God, do you eat anything normal?"

"That is normal. Have you ever had it? It's delicious."

"No. Let me rephrase the question. Do you eat anything I might possibly have in this kitchen? Like eggs? Bacon? By the way, we have good bacon here, not that awful stuff you Americans try to pass off as bacon. I had some on a trip to New York City, and it was bloody awful."

"Lord Grace Viscount," I say, teasing him, "I'll have you know our bacon is fantastic."

He laughs. "I think that's the first time I've been called Lord

Grace Viscount."

We reach the bottom of the steps. "It won't be the last time," I say, lifting my own brow up. "Now what is wrong with our bacon?"

"Besides the fact that it's disgusting?"

I follow him to the kitchen, which still blows me away with the sheer size of it. It's been updated, of course, but I can only imagine how it was here back in the 1700s, with a full staff working on preparing lavish meals for the lord and lady of the house and all their country guests.

"It's not disgusting," I insist.

"It's nearly all fat," Phillip counters. He moves around a large kitchen island and faces me. "Ours is mostly meat. A far superior product."

"We'll see about that," I say.

Truth be told, I could care less about eating bacon. It's not even my favorite breakfast food.

But I will talk about bacon endlessly if it means I can keep talking to Phillip. I want to make him laugh and forget whatever is making him be so serious all the time.

"Okay. Let's say the kitchen is yours," Phillip says, spreading his arms wide. "What would you make besides the two things you've already said. If you didn't have to count calories or fat or any of that stuff. What would make you happy on a Saturday morning? Unless you are a health nut, and a tofu scramble would be your choice."

I reach up and tuck a lock of my hair behind my ear. "Oh, no, I'm all about moderation. I think my perfect Saturday breakfast would be a big plate of Nutella-stuffed french toast. You can't skimp on the Nutella. You have to layer it thick in there. Then I top it with powdered sugar and maple syrup. It's decadent and sinful, and I need to change into pants with an elastic band after eating it, but it's so amazing. That with a cup of coffee with a lot of cream in it. That's perfect."

"Sounds perfectly balanced," he says dryly. "What's powdered sugar?"

"You've never heard of that?" I ask, surprised. "Surely, you have. You know that white sugar that looks like powder? You see it sprinkled on baked goods and cake?"

Phillip's face lights up in recognition. "Oh, icing sugar."

"Icing sugar? Is that what you call it here?"

"Yes," he says.

Suddenly, I have an idea. Normally, I spring my wild bursts of creative ideas on the children I'm caring for, but as I study Phillip, I want to make him do something spontaneous and fun.

He needs it, my gut tells me.

"Phillip?" I ask.

"I'm sorry, I believe you gave me a proper title this morning."

The butterflies shift in my stomach. "I'm sorry, Lord Grace Viscount?"

He grins. My God, he's beautiful when he allows that smile to break through.

"That's better. Yes?"

"I think we should have a breakfast battle this morning."

"A what?"

"Like a competition. We can each make our idea of the perfect breakfast—well, as long I have the ingredients here to make french toast—and we'll let Rose and John and the children judge it. We can get points for taste and presentation. The prize will be the title of best breakfast chef of Mooreton House. What do you think? Oh, wait! We can have something to nibble on now, but when the children get up, we can split them up to be our

46

sous chefs! Now that would be so much fun."

Phillip stares at me with a surprised look on his face. I wait for him to tell me I've lost my mind.

"Well, you see," he says, reaching up and raking a hand through his golden blond hair, "normally breakfast is the time I catch up on emails and sort out my work for the day."

I study him carefully. The seriousness is back in his eyes. I wonder if he worked last night. He probably did. And now he's laying out a plan to work on a Saturday.

But why is Phillip the only one working? If his father is the earl, why isn't he running the family business? How is this all put on Phillip's young shoulders?

There are so many questions I have, but they are questions I have no business asking.

"I understand," I say, nodding. "I know you have a lot to do."

He's silent for a moment. "I do."

With his words, I'm reminded that I am overstepping my boundaries this morning. I'm laughing and joking with Rose's *brother.* What would she have to say if she knew I called him "Lord Grace Viscount?"

I cringe as I imagine the response to that.

"Pardon me," he says, getting up and moving over to the cabinets.

Embarrassment sweeps through me. Laughing and joking with him is one thing, but the nanny creating a nickname for the aristocratic viscount uncle and challenging him to a cook-off is another. I definitely went a bridge too far this time.

Er, two bridges, actually.

I'm about to apologize, but Phillip opens a cabinet and speaks first.

"Hmm."

I don't say anything. I should go about my own business now and grab some breakfast before the kids are up scrambling around and asking for something to eat and cartoons on the TV.

I head over to the fridge and am weighing out whether to apologize or merely let the subject drop when Phillip speaks again.

"You are going to be at a disadvantage," he says.

My hand freezes on the fridge handle. I turn around. Phillip's back is to me, but he's poking around in the cabinet as if he's looking for something.

"I'm sorry?" I ask.

"We don't have icing sugar. Pity, you're going to go down in flames on your first challenge."

My pulse jumps. Phillip turns around and cocks an eyebrow at me.

"Come on now," he says slowly, his voice low and sexy. "It's not quite a *duel*, so it's a tame challenge, but I'll accept it anyway. On one condition, that is."

Every nerve I have jumps. "And what is that?"

"I pick the next one."

Chapter Five

I have been on the job less than forty-eight hours, and I'm already on my second shower to scrub away the mess of being the Palmerstons' nanny.

I wrap a thick, plush white towel around me and step out of my en suite bathroom. The breakfast cook-off was a great success to start the day. At first, the children all wanted to be on Team Phillip—until I showed them I was cooking with Nutella that would need to be sampled. Then they all abandoned Phillip for my team. I smile. Of course, when the children voted, our french toast won in a crushing landslide to Phillip's hideous-looking plate that included beans and the black pudding that I don't even want to know the ingredients of.

Rose and John arrived to find their kitchen in chaos, with chattering children and a nanny with Nutella on her face and her hair wound up and held back in a messy knot with a pencil—a trick that delighted the kids and even left Phillip looking amused. I don't know what surprised them more—that we were a whirl of laughter and activity, or that Phillip had joined us. The strange thing is, when John teased Phillip that this was out of character for him, Phillip's face completely changed. My heart caught as his smile faded. His expression became serious, and the light went out of his eyes. When Rose asked if he wanted to go to the farmer's market with us, he declined, saying he had to work, and I haven't seen him since.

We, of course, traipsed off and loaded up on all kinds of vegetables and fresh fruits, including strawberries that I got to sample, which were the best ones I have ever had in my life. When I asked Rose and John what they were going to do with all these vegetables, they blinked. Good God, it was like they thought the food would magically become dinner if they stared at it long enough. I offered to make dinner tonight, something California-inspired, and they eagerly agreed. To be honest, I couldn't bear the idea of another night of cod sticks, so I was relieved they said yes.

After the market, we decided to feed the ducks at a nearby pond. That is when Byron, running gleefully close to the water, didn't heed my warnings and got way too close to the edge. I sprinted after him, lost my footing in some mud, and ended up tumbling into the pond. The children thought this was great fun, Rose turned bright red and offered a stream of apologies, and John said Byron was going to be in time out as soon as we got home.

So, after scrubbing pond scum off my body and out of my hair, I'm ready to face the rest of my day.

Hopefully, it will not include another shower.

I step into my room and go over to my bed, where I carefully laid out my second outfit of the day: a pair of skinny black jeans, a long-sleeved chambray shirt, and leopard-print tennis shoes. I always make sure I dress in comfortable clothes that can get dirty and are modest. No scoop-neck tops that are impossible to be modest in when bending over, for example. This outfit strikes just the right note of cute and practical.

I remove the bath sheet from around my body, placing it on the bench at the end of the bed, and pick up my panties. I slip into those, and I'm about to reach for my bra when the door to my room flings open, banging against the wall, and I shriek loudly as I find myself face-to-face with a gaggle of elderly people, staring agog at me.

I fumble for the towel, holding it up to my body, horrified that all these strangers have just seen me almost totally naked.

"Wh-what are you doing here?" I sputter, flabbergasted. "This ... this is my room!"

"Connie, I know I told you these tours were dull," says an elderly man with a distinctly Midwestern accent. "I take it back now." He grins creepily at me.

"Oh, is this a private room?" another woman says, looking around. "And are you American? You don't sound English."

"Vivi," a woman wearing a huge straw hat says, "it's like *Downton Abbey!* Maybe she's an American heiress rescuing this crumbling pile of bricks!"

"McKenna! Are you—" Phillip shouts, bursting into the room, but his words die on his lips as soon as he enters it. He stops dead in his tracks, staring at me, his mouth hanging open as soon as he sees me holding a towel against my nearly naked body.

Oh my God! I feel myself turn red from head to toe, much like the berries we picked up at the market this morning.

"Um ..." Phillip starts out, staring at me for a moment. But then he blinks and tears his gaze away from me to the tourists. "I'm sorry, this is a private wing of the house that is not on the tour. I'll escort you out now."

"We paid thirty bucks for this, I want to see all the rooms in the house," a man with a large camera hung around his neck declares.

"Connie, look at the bed. Isn't it gorgeous?" a woman asks, picking up her phone to take a picture.

"You *will* be leaving now," Phillip repeats, his voice going a bit lower as he steps in front of the camera.

"So rude!" a woman who is wearing a shirt with—good God, with a *cat butt* on it—sniffs.

"I will refund your money as soon as we are downstairs," Phillip says curtly.

"One question before we go," Cat Butt woman says. "Have any mistresses had this room? That would be some spicy dirt."

"No," Phillip says through clenched teeth. "Now please leave."

He holds the door open for them, and they reluctantly head out. Then one woman turns around and stares sympathetically at me.

"Dearie, you might want to cover up a bit better," she says, her voice with an air of discretion in it.

What?

I glance down.

OH MOTHER OF GOD.

My left nipple is completely visible and uncovered by the towel.

I shift the towel to cover it up, but it's too late.

Phillip has seen my boob.

I need to die now.

"Out!" Phillip snaps, losing it. He gets them all out and shuts the door behind him.

I cringe the second the door is closed. Then I run over and turn the key in the lock for good measure. Mortification fills every cell in my body.

Phillip has seen me nearly naked. Of all people, I didn't want him to see me like this! I quickly get dressed, throwing on clothing and thinking of all the ways Phillip has seen me since I started this job yesterday. The list is beyond humiliating. He's seen me fall in a cow pasture. Phillip has driven me around with manure in my hair. He's dealt with my ugly crying and snotting on his shirt. The pencil in my hair was of my choosing, but not exactly a stylish look. He's seen me with Nutella on my nose, and now, holding a towel against me and completely oblivious that my left nipple was practically waving at him.

I close my eyes. I came to England to find myself. Instead, I find myself rolling from one humiliation to another with the viscount as my audience.

I open my eyes and exhale. Well, there's no avoiding this one. As soon as I've dried my hair and reapplied my makeup, I'll have to go downstairs and relieve Rose, who is serving lunch to the children while I recover from my "tiny little slip into the pond."

I section my long hair into clips so I can dry it one area at a time. But first, I redo my skin routine, and just as I'm applying sunscreen to my neck, there's a knock on my door.

"McKenna?" Phillip calls out.

I stare back at myself, with my hair looking ridiculous and the white zinc sunscreen not totally blended into my neck, and give up. There's no hope of ever being seen as normal in Phillip's eyes, so why even try to take a few minutes to do it now?

I enter the bedroom and walk over to the door. I turn the key in the lock and open it, stepping aside so Phillip can enter.

To his credit, he doesn't seem fazed by my hair. But then again, he might be thinking about my nipple, who knows.

"I'm so sorry about that," Phillip says. "Are you okay?"

"Yes. They scared me to death, but I'm okay."

53

Phillip rakes a hand through his hair. "I . . . I'm sorry I didn't tell you to cover up your ... your breast. I ... I didn't know if I should acknowledge it or ignore it or if I said something, I would be drawing attention to it. I didn't handle that very well."

I stare at him, dumbstruck. He's apologizing for not telling me to cover up?

He's not real. Phillip is too gorgeous and thoughtful and smart to be a real man.

"Please, it's not your fault I can't manage to cover up my own boob," I say. "You think I'd notice something like that, but no, what did I notice? That a woman was wearing a shirt with a cat butt on it. So, I don't want to know what that says about me."

Phillip looks relieved. Then he grins, and everything else melts away when I see that smile of his.

"That definitely wins for shirt of the day," he teases. Then he clears his throat. "I take it Rose didn't tell you to lock your door when you're here?"

I shake my head. Phillip rolls his eyes.

"Typical. Right. Well, tourists have a habit of either wandering off on their own or thinking it's their right to see everything they want to see. So, what happened to you happens from time to time in this wing of the house, because it's one staircase away from the tour rooms."

I furrow my brow. "That's awful that people don't respect those boundaries. I would *hate* living in a place where tourists were running wild. It would never feel like a real home, but an attraction."

A shadow crosses Phillip's face. The smile evaporates on his lips, and with a pang, I realize what I just said to him.

"Oh, Phillip, I'm sorry, that's not what I meant," I try to backpedal, as this is his home when he's in the country.

It's not only his home, however. It's a home he inherited and has *no choice* but to live in when he comes out to manage the estate.

Phillip puts up a hand before I can say anything else. "I understand. More than you know."

Oh, my stupid mouth!. I want to take it all back, but Phillip clears his throat before I can think of a way to do so.

"I should get back to work. I hope you enjoy the rest of your day," he says softly.

Then he retreats and shuts the door behind him.

I stare at the door, anxiety clawing at my stomach. I struck a nerve with my insensitive comment, and Phillip pulled away the second I did.

And the idea of Phillip pulling away makes my stomach churn even further.

Wait a minute. Why am I feeling this way? I barely know Phillip. I shouldn't care if I see him once a day or once a week or never again for the rest of the summer. He's a viscount, the brother of my employer, and I'm the nanny. There are boundary lines here that will never be crossed.

But they already have on my side.

I'm attracted to Phillip. Lord, more than I've ever been attracted to any man. I feel comfortable with him. I've been vulnerable with him, cried on him, and laughed with him. When I had one of my silly ideas for the children, he jumped right in with no hesitation.

And this should terrify me.

Never mind the big, huge line of being proper with my boss's brother, which would no doubt get me fired on the spot if I dared to cross it.

But more terrifying is the idea of possibly falling for him.

I go back to the bathroom and stare at my reflection. I've always kept men at bay. While I know my father found love again with my mom, I can't imagine how his heart was broken when Anna—my mum—died. I never wanted to know that kind of pain, of having a broken heart. I remember seeing my Aunt Emily, when she was in her twenties, sob her heart out to my mom over a guy who broke her heart at USC. Like gut-wrenching, wailing, her-heart-was-truly-broken sobs. I remember watching as a child and thinking I would never want to cry like that for a man or have love cause me that kind of pain.

And truth be told, I never met any who seemed worth that risk.

Until I found Phillip Coventry standing over me in a pasture.

I close my eyes, exhale, and slowly open them. The light I saw in my brown eyes earlier this morning is gone. I feel dull. I hate that I upset him. And I hate the fact that I want to be near him.

Right. Well, I didn't come here to fall in love. Or get a crush on a viscount that will never be reciprocated. I came here to be a nanny and to find myself. Tomorrow, we head back to London, and as soon as I'm settled, I'm going to let my British aunt, Grace, know my days off and see if I can meet her for lunch or dinner. We've done some video chats on the social media app Connectivity, and she's been so wonderful and welcoming to me. She said when we meet, she is going to give me the biggest hug and tell me all about my mum.

See? That is why I'm here.

It has nothing to do with Phillip.

From the look on his face when he retreated today, I doubt I'll be seeing much of him, anyway. I don't know when he's going back to London. I know he has his own flat there, and I'm sure he'll be back hitting the nightclubs in no time and will only swing by on occasion to visit his nieces and nephews.

I should be relieved by this reality.

But instead, I feel sad.

And somehow, I'll have to find a way to move past it.

Chapter Six

It's a glorious afternoon in Hyde Park, with the sun shining and puffy white clouds dotting the sky. I smile as I watch the Palmerston children run around the playground with glee, exploring the climbing frames and slides of the South Carriage Playground.

I sit at a picnic table and watch them, taking a sip of my afternoon coffee and enjoying the views of the lake—called the Serpentine—and playing fields from my spot. Layla is chatting with another girl while they go up and down the slide. Byron and Louis are going back and forth on the climbing frames, and Pippa is happy blowing the bubbles I gave her.

It's Friday afternoon. We've been in London for a week, and I'm off for the weekend after five o'clock this evening. I've been able to explore so many things in the city with the children, and every one of them has been a treat for me. We went to the Tate Modern museum of art on Monday, where I had the children find a pose in the gallery and then mimic it so I could take their picture. To carry over the art theme, the next day, we went on a color walk throughout Knightsbridge, with each child responsible for finding items of a particular color. Yesterday, I took them to the London Transport Museum, and I think that will be a once a week stop for us. The kids loved all the buses and trains and signs on display, and they didn't want to leave when it was time to go.

The outings, of course, were scheduled around Layla's tennis lesson on Tuesday, Pippa's dance lesson on Wednesday, and the boys' football practice this morning. Needless to say, they aren't the only ones who are tired by the end of the day. If we aren't going, we're learning and creating and doing, and I'm looking forward to having my first weekend off.

I pause for a moment. Even more so tonight, because I'm meeting my aunt and cousins for the first time.

Nerves sweep over me, as they do every time I think about this meeting. While I've spoken to all of them on Connectivity Video Chat, there's something about meeting them in person that makes me anxious. Will we all get along as well as we are now? Or will I be an uncomfortable, painful reminder of what my aunt lost when that car accident happened in Essex twenty-two years ago?

I take another sip from my Rifle Paper Co. coffee tumbler and trace my fingertip over the floral pattern on it after I set it back down on the table. I have so many mixed emotions about this evening. I'm so desperate to find out about my mum. I want to know if I'm like her in any way. If we share some passions and interests. I want to know about her favorite places in London and go to them, to see if I can feel that connection to her.

I want to know Anna.

If I know her, I feel as if I can finally know myself.

"McKenna, look at this bubble!" Pippa calls out, interrupting my thoughts and pointing to a big, soapy bubble drifting up in the air.

I gasp in delight. "Pippa! It's huge! Did you really make

that?"

"I did!" she cries happily.

"That's amazing," I say, smiling at her.

I scan the playground once again, making sure I count all four of my charges. Yep, all four accounted for, not fighting, all playing, and nobody is bleeding. So far, so good at Hyde Park.

My mind goes back to this evening. I can take the tube from Knightsbridge to Chiswick, where Grace has an apartment that's a short walk from the underground station. She said she will make a dinner with my mum and grandparents' favorite foods, and my cousins, Imogen and Cleo, will share dishes they love, too. She called it a collection of Brown family favorites.

I swallow. These people are my family. That's such a big thought to digest, when all I've ever known is my American family.

I wonder if we can bond as a family, too.

I let my thoughts drift back to the family I'm with now, the Palmerstons. I've gotten settled into my room at the historic Georgian townhouse that the Palmerstons call home in Knightsbridge. The home is on Montpelier Square and was built in the nineteenth century. It has been in the Palmerston family ever since it was built. One of the remaining properties that the Phillip in the portrait managed to save.

And that the current Phillip has to find a way to maintain and keep within the family.

I haven't seen Phillip since I made that horrible remark about Mooreton House. My face feels hot every time I revisit that conversation and how I wish I could take those words back. I have fought the urge to ask Rose about him. I don't even know where he is. Rose told me Phillip keeps a hideous flat in Mayfair, one that is wretchedly small—not fit for a Coventry to live in.

I smirk. Well, that might be true in her eyes, now that I've seen Mooreton House and have spent a week exploring a Georgian townhouse that has a gym, media room, heated floors, six bedrooms, and more marble than I've ever seen in my life, but I have a suspicion Phillip's flat is probably not wretched at all.

I'm sure she's wondering why Phillip even lives there in the first place. Technically, the townhome on Montpelier Square will be his someday. I'm sure Rose and John were given the townhome because they have a big family and Phillip is single. His parents stay in the guest room when they come to London, but according to Rose, they have a home in Capri that they favor and spend nearly all their time there.

I can't help but wonder if Phillip has to manage that home in Italy, too. His youngest sister, Lady Georgina, is making her own money as a model and social media influencer, according to Rose, who's quite sure she's on the verge of dropping out of university, much to Phillip's dismay. But I don't know if that means Lady Georgina is self-sufficient, either.

And if that is another worry added to Phillip's plate.

I watch as Louis runs gleefully across the playground, a huge smile lighting up his face, with nothing but fun on his little mind. My heart catches, as I want the same for Phillip. I want him to have more of the joy and carefree abandon that Louis has now. I want him to smile, to laugh, to do things just for him, because my gut tells me he doesn't. Except for going to nightclubs, which makes no sense to me. That doesn't seem to match the Phillip I met at all.

But I don't know Phillip, I remind myself. *I'm still getting to know who Viscount Brookstone really is. And the truth is, I might never even see him again to learn anything else about him.*

Now a gloomy feeling creeps in, kicking my anxiety to the

curb and taking residence within me. I might never see him again, and although it shouldn't bother me in the least, it does.

I try not to think about it as I play with the children. Time goes by quickly, and soon, it's time to head back.

"Okay, it's time for us to go home now," I say. "Let me pick up my backpack, and we'll go."

"Noooooooooooooooooooo," Byron cries.

"Just five more minutes!" Layla counters.

I shake my head. "No, no, we need to go home now. But I have some snacks waiting for you!"

That seems to be the magic word. Before I know it, they are rounded up and we are all walking out of Hyde Park together.

As we head back toward Montpelier Square, I come up with a counting game for them to play on the way. We count buses and yellow cars and black cabs, and I give Layla the extra challenge of doing simple math.

"Why do I have to do maths?" Layla asks, almost crossly.

"Because you are the oldest, and you know so much more about maths," I say, building up her confidence. "I asked you because I *know* you can do it."

Her eyes regard me with new interest. "Oh, yes, I can!"

I give her some more problems to solve, and she gets them all right straight away. Layla is whip smart, that is for sure. I need to find more ways to keep her challenged, engaged, and feeling special for being someone other than the big sister of triplets.

Soon we are back home, and once the children step through the doorway, I have all their shoes taken off and have marched them downstairs to wash their hands. Once that task is finished, I bring them to the kitchen, where I find Rose sipping a glass of white wine and leafing through a fashion magazine at the massive kitchen island.

"Mummy!" the children yell, racing up to her. Rose gets down off her seat, and soon she is enveloped in hugs and kisses and tales about what happened at the park.

"Oh, what a lovely time you all had with McKenna today," Rose exclaims.

I smile as she asks them all kinds of questions about what we did in the park. I open the refrigerator and take out the stuff I prepared for snacks last night.

"If you all will take a seat at the table, I will bring you your snacks," I say cheerfully.

"What are we having?" Louis asks, scrambling into a chair.

"Very special apples," I say, putting several containers of cream cheese on the countertop.

"Is that why you had me order sprinkles?" Rose asks, grinning at me.

"Mummy! Can we watch TV?" Pippa calls out. "Can we watch Peppa?"

"Yes," Rose says, reaching for the remote and turning on the TV. She scrolls through her options until she finds *Peppa Pig* and then puts it on. Then she moves around to my side of the island, looking down at what I have out. "What's all this?"

I begin slicing the apples, and then carefully cutting out the cores. "I'm going to make them look like frosted donuts," I say. "I made icing with cream cheese that is sweetened up a little, which I will use to frost them, and then I'll put the sprinkles on top."

"That is genius," Rose says, a look of delight on her face. "I knew I made the right decision to hire you!"

"Thank you," I say, smiling.

"So, tonight you meet the British side of the family?" Rose asks.

I carefully cut out a circle with my knife. This would be so much easier with a corer or small circle cookie cutter, but alas, no such items are to be found in this kitchen.

"Yes, I'm very excited about it," I say. "And nervous."

"I think that's totally normal," Rose says. "Would you like a glass of wine before you go?"

I laugh. "No. Thank you, though."

"McKenna, may I have a drink?" Byron calls out.

"How do we ask?" I remind him.

"Please," he says.

While Rose pours out juice and sets out plates, I open the containers of spreads–one is honey, one is chocolate, and there's a pink one I made with strawberry puree. I spread the apple rings so they look like iced donuts, add the sprinkles, and bring them over to the table. The children are instantly delighted with what they see.

"They look like donuts," Louis says.

"I love pink ones," Pippa pipes up.

"They are apple donuts," I say, putting the plate down in the middle of the table.

"I want a chocolate one," Byron says.

"How do we ask for something, Master Byron?" I ask.

"Please. May I please have a chocolate one?"

"Yes, you may, thank you for asking so nicely," I say.

Within minutes, they are snacking and chatting away and watching TV. Rose and I hang out in the kitchen, and I'm always surprised at how much she talks to me. None of my previous employers really did, at least, not about things outside of the children. She asks for my opinion on a lipstick color and what she should order for dinner tonight. She shows me some things out of the fashion magazine that caught her eye and some editorial fashions that we both giggle about.

After snack time ends, I'm about to take the children upstairs for some reading time before dinner, but Rose stops me.

"Go on," she says. "You have worked non-stop since last Friday, even though I offered you two days off this week. I've got this. And I know how to order a pizza."

"Really?" I ask, biting my lip.

"Yes, really," she says, laughing. "Go on."

"Thank you, Rose," I say, smiling gratefully at her.

"You're welcome."

I head up the four flights of stairs to my room on the top floor, one floor above the children's rooms. I step into my closet and flick through my clothing, deciding to wear a dress for this evening. I choose a ruffled wrap chambray dress I got from Nordstrom before I left for London. I'll wear that with some tennis shoes, so I can walk from the tube to my aunt's flat. I'll also pair it with a light white cardigan so I'm comfortable by the time I leave in the evening.

I feel the butterflies begin as I start to get ready, as I want to make a good impression on the family I'm meeting for the first time. I dry my hair, opting to wear it down and straight. I apply my makeup, putting bronzer on my cheeks to bring back that California glow. I put on my initial pendant necklace, the one with an M, and then grab my perfume and spritz it on my neck and wrists.

Okay. It's time. I pick up my purse off my dresser, as well as the bottle of wine I brought from California for this occasion, and head down the stairs. I could take the elevator, of course, but if we're having a massive spread of food tonight, I need all the extra steps I can fit in.

I stop on the third floor, but the children's rooms are empty.

I was going to say goodbye before I left, so I'll go down to the lower ground floor to see if they are in the kitchen. Once I reach that level, I hear giggling from the kitchen. I smile. That's Louis's bubbly, joyful laugh.

"Do it again!" he squeals.

I reach the kitchen but stop dead in my tracks at the sight in front of me.

It's Phillip.

My heart leaps inside my chest. The butterflies appear in my stomach for a new reason. He's holding Louis up high in the air, tossing him and catching him, and he has the biggest smile on his face.

"I'm next!" Pippa pleads, clasping onto his jeans.

"McKenna!" Byron says. "Are you staying for pizza?"

Phillip turns around when he sees me, and I swear I can't breathe.

"No, loves, I came to wish you good evening," I say, smiling at them. "I am going out tonight." I pause. "Hello, Phillip. It's good to see you."

"McKenna," he says, his expression serious.

Inside, I wilt. I want that smiling, joyful Phillip back. And I hate that now, that Phillip fades in my presence.

"Do you have a date?" Layla asks.

"I'm meeting my family," I explain.

I glance at Phillip, who doesn't seem surprised by this news, which I find odd. He knows what this means to me—I'd expect him to have more of a reaction than that. Unless my comment about his family estate totally put him off me, but if that is the case, that's stupid. Was it a thoughtless thing for me to say? Yes. Unforgiveable? I would think not.

I grow irritated as that thought takes hold in my head.

"Did you work out the tube timetable to Chiswick?" John asks. He has come home from work and is in the kitchen along with Rose. "Want me to have a look at it for you?"

"No, but thank you for asking. I feel as if I know where I'm going. But I'm leaving early in case I get mixed up."

"No," Phillip says, his eyes lingering on my face. "There's a better option."

I stare at him in confusion. "What? The tube is cheaper than an Uber."

"Me. I'll drive you," Phillip says. "If you will let me, that is."

Chapter Seven

I stare at Phillip in complete shock. He wants to drive me to my family's flat. After disappearing off the face of the earth, he's here, on a Friday night, offering to escort me to my first-ever meeting with the people who knew and loved my mum.

"Oh, no, thank you for your offer, but I'm fine taking the tube," I say, shaking my head. "You don't have to go out of your way for me."

"Don't do it for you," John pipes up. "Do it for us. Keep him out of the clubs tonight."

Phillip scowls. "If I was planning to go to a club tonight, I wouldn't be here."

"I really am fine taking the tube," I insist.

Phillip shifts his attention back to me. "Please. Let me drive you. It's only around ten minutes from here."

I feel my breath catch. I have no chance of riding the tube now, not as I stare up into the handsome, familiar face I've found comfort in from the moment I first saw him. It's terrifying to admit, but I need Phillip's steadiness right now.

"Okay. Thank you," I say.

Phillip nods. He turns to Rose. "Don't worry about me for dinner. I'll have leftovers when I come back, or I'll grab a takeaway."

Rose nods. "Good luck, McKenna. Although I know they will love you as much as we already do."

Her kind words nearly make me tear up. "Thank you."

"Let's go," Phillip says.

He escorts me back up the stairs and to the front door. We walk in silence outside to his car, which is parked down the street. Phillip opens the passenger door for me, and I thank him and slip inside. He moves around to the driver's side, and before I can say a word, he asks me for the address to put into his navigation system.

"No," I say. "Not until I've had the chance to say something to you."

Phillip's eyes widen in surprise. "What?"

I swallow. "Phillip, I'm so sorry about what I said to you at Mooreton House."

His brow furrows. "What? What are you talking about?"

"When I said I couldn't imagine living there," I admit, my face growing hot with embarrassment. "That was rude and something I said as someone who simply isn't used to having a home that is also a tourist spot. I've thought about it since it came out of my mouth, and I wished I would have the opportunity to apologize to you. Now that I do, I had to say that first."

A look of amazement filters across his handsome face. "You were really worried about this, weren't you?"

I nod. "I was. I'm so sorry I was so insensitive."

He looks away from me, staring out of the windshield to the street straight ahead of us.

"Did you think I stayed away from you after that on purpose?" he asks.

"Yes," I say, the words barely audible to my own ears.

"Then you would be correct," he says, his voice low. "But not because I was angry. Far from it." He exhales and rakes a hand through his blond hair. "Christ. I don't know how to explain it to you when I can't even explain it to myself."

My heart pounds furiously inside my chest. If he didn't care what I thought, if he didn't care what I said, if he had no interest in me, he wouldn't avoid me. That thought never would have crossed his mind in the first place. So, if I hadn't insulted him, if I didn't make him angry, my comment somehow hurt him. If I didn't matter to him, he wouldn't care what I thought or said about his home.

I can't breathe as my brain processes this information. What I say matters to him. Phillip cares about what I think for one reason only.

Phillip cares about me.

"McKenna, this is a conversation for later," he says, breaking through my thoughts. "I promise we'll talk about it, but this isn't the time. Not when you are about to meet your British family for the first time."

"You promise we'll come back to this?" I ask.

Phillip turns to face me, his vivid blue eyes locking on my face. "Yes, I promise."

I nod, believing him.

He starts the car, and I give him the address to Grace's flat. Once he enters that, Phillip pulls out into the street, and silence fills the space between us.

"How are you feeling?" he asks.

I stare out the window, watching the Georgian-style homes go by. "I couldn't sleep last night. I've had an upset stomach all day. I mean, I've met them all on video chat, so they aren't strangers to me, but I can't help but worry that it will be awkward in person. Or worse …" I stop and clear my throat. "I won't feel my mum."

Phillip immediately moves a hand to cover mine. It's warm and rough and strong, and as he gives my hand a reassuring squeeze, strength flows through me.

"I hope you find what you are looking for tonight, but even if you don't, you're going to be okay," he says.

"I know you're right. And it's unreasonable of me to put all these expectations on this meeting, that suddenly I'll meet my mum's sister and my cousins, and I'll feel as if all my missing pieces are complete."

Phillip is quiet for a moment. "Is that how you feel? As if something is missing?"

"Yes," I admit to him. "Like there's a part of me that needs to be unlocked by learning more about my mum."

His hand remains on mine as he drives, his thumb now idly stroking across the back of my hand in a soothing motion. Goosebumps erupt over my skin from this gentle touch and the way he's caring for me right now.

Before we know it, Phillip is turning onto my aunt's street. I grow both excited and queasy at the same time. As the navigation device announces it's the next house on the right, I nearly feel lightheaded.

"This is it," Phillip says. "Take as long as you need before going inside."

"I'm scared."

"I know you are. I would be, too."

I turn to him, and I see nothing but strength when I look at him. Phillip is compassionate and kind and solid. The most grounded man I have ever known. I need him. I need to do this

71

with him, to have someone by my side who can help me deal with the emotional roller coaster I'm about to venture on.

I never would have dreamed of asking anyone to share this experience with me.

Until I met Phillip.

And the words escape my lips before I can stop them.

"Will you go in with me?" I ask.

"Me?" he says, his eyes wide in shock. "You want me to meet your family?"

Oh, crap. I never should have asked him that. All the lines I should be creating between myself and Phillip disappear when he's in my presence.

He's holding my hand and comforting me, yet this is too personal of a step. It's too forward. For god's sake, I work for Rose an—

"Are you sure?" he asks, interrupting my thoughts.

"No, I'm sorry, I never should have asked that," I say, quickly withdrawing my hand from his. "It's completely inappropriate."

"I've seen your breast. I think we're beyond that," Phillip says, cocking an eyebrow.

"*What?*" I shriek. "It's not like I whipped off my top for you, Lord Grace Viscount!"

A huge grin lights up his face. "There, that's better."

I manage a small laugh. It is better to laugh right now.

"But McKenna, I would be honored," he says, his voice low, "if you want me to be a part of your journey. I will go inside with you if that is what you want. I will sit next to you and hold your hand and not say anything at all, but I will be there with you."

Oh, no. I think I might ugly cry, and I haven't even seen my family yet. My eyes begin to swim with tears, and I bite down hard on my lower lip in an effort to keep back the sob that is threatening to break loose from my throat.

"Oh, no, no, I know this look," Phillip says quickly. "You save that ugly cry for your aunt and your cousins. Don't waste it on a *Lord Grace Viscount.*"

I can't help it. I laugh, and he chuckles.

I clear my throat. "I would like you to be there with me."

"Then I will go in with you. Whenever you are ready."

I reach inside my purse and grab my pack of tissues, taking one and dabbing my eyes. I take a few breaths of air in and out.

"Okay," I say quietly.

We get out of the Jaguar, and Phillip walks next to me on the sidewalk. My heart is beating out of my chest—I swear I can feel the fabric of my dress moving in rhythm with it, it's beating that hard. I slowly walk up the steps, nerves growing steeper with every step. Finally, we're at the front door, and I freeze before ringing the doorbell.

"Take your time," Phillip says, putting his hand lightly on the small of my back. "There's no rush."

I nod. Then I gather up all my courage and ring the doorbell.

I can hear some noises behind the door, and I can't think, as the blood is rushing to my head. The door is opened, and I'm face-to-face with my Aunt Grace.

Tears fill her eyes the second she sees me, and my own eyes fill with tears, too.

"Oh, my God, you look so much like Anna," she says, her voice breaking. "I thought so in our chats, but seeing you here in person? It's like looking at Anna again."

Then she takes me into her arms and gives me a huge hug, and we both begin to cry. Grace puts her hands on my arms and takes a step back from me, searching my face.

"I hope looking at me doesn't upset you," I say with a thick voice.

She shakes her head. "Not at all. You bear a striking resemblance to her, but you are McKenna, not Anna."

"Grace, I hope you don't mind, but I brought a friend with me this evening," I say. "This is Phillip Coventry."

Phillip extends his hand, and Grace shakes it, taking him in with surprise.

"Oh, of course, any friend of yours is welcome here," she says, smiling at us. "Please, come in."

Grace ushers us into a comfortable living room, filled with bookcases, cushy sofas, and throw pillows, and I find my cousins standing there with eager expressions on their faces. I present the wine to Grace, and she happily accepts it, and then clears her throat.

"I know we've all met online, but let's do this properly. McKenna, this is my eldest daughter, Imogen," she says, introducing me to my cousin who has bright pink hair and tattoo sleeves.

"Hello." I extend my hand to her. "It's so good to finally meet you in person."

"Same," she replies, flashing me a beautiful smile.

"And this is Cleo," Grace says. I smile as a petite woman with layered, sandy-brown hair shakes my hand.

"So good to have you here," she says happily.

"This," I say, turning around to Phillip, "is my good friend Phillip Coventry. He was kind enough to offer to escort me this evening."

Phillip quickly extends his hand and greets everyone, and I see the curious look in all of their eyes as to who he really is in my life.

Which is a great question. A question I can't even answer myself.

"Please, welcome, and have a seat," Grace says. "Would you like some drinks? A glass of water? A soft drink? I'll save this wine for dinner, if that's okay."

Phillip and I both decline the offer and sit together on the sofa. I rest my hands in my lap, anxiously twisting my rings around my fingers.

"I'm so glad you decided to meet us," Grace begins, smiling at me from the oversized chair near the bookcases. "First, I want to say, I did what I thought was best by staying back. I know how much your father loved Anna, but I also know how much he loves Samantha. And oh, how that woman loves you, McKenna. I couldn't have asked for anyone better to be your mother if it couldn't have been Anna. I told them I wanted to step back from your life to uncomplicate it. I didn't want the past you never knew crowding your future, so I promised her I would never seek you out. That if you wanted to meet us, it had to be when you were an adult. Maybe that was too extreme, but I did it with your best interest in mind, my dear."

"Thank you," I say. "I always wondered about my family, but I was too afraid to bring up Mum. The accident. It was so painful for Dad. While growing up, he always made sure I knew I had a mom and a mum, and Mummy was in heaven and is my angel, when I was old enough to truly hear the story, he spoke it that one time. As if he could only open that box of pain once and relive it for my sake."

Grace reaches for a tissue and dabs her eyes. "He loved Anna with his whole heart."

I swallow hard. "My mom did the best she could to talk to me about my mum, but there are things only you would know,

Grace, as her sister. I ... I–I want to know my mum."

My voice breaks, and Phillip immediately puts his arm around my shoulders and draws me into his chest. Imogen grabs a tissue, and Cleo clears her throat.

"Let me tell you about Anna," Grace says gently.

* * *

Hours later, after many laughs and tears and eating more food than any human should in one sitting, I say goodbye to my British family. I now know my mum's favorite places in London, and I plan to see them all. I learned my love of the ocean comes from my mum, as well as the way I ugly cry, which I found interesting and amusing. I looked at pictures and watched videos and saw a beautiful, dark-haired woman, with the same splash of freckles across her nose and cheeks as I do, affectionately dote on her husband and cradle me lovingly in her arms.

We all agreed to keep in touch, but I honestly don't know how often I will see them. As I heard stories about my mum and my grandparents who perished in the crash, I didn't feel the connection I had so desperately hoped I would feel. I felt as if I was sitting in a living room with very nice strangers, sharing stories and memories about the biggest stranger in my life—my own mum.

As we say goodbye and Grace closes the door behind us, I can't help but think a door has closed on my past, too. I found out everything I could, but one fact remains.

I didn't find the part of me that was missing.

I blink back tears as Phillip escorts me to the car, his hand on the small of my back as we walk into the dark night. He never left my side this evening, and I was so grateful he was there. He was either holding me, handing me tissues, or squeezing my hand. This man, this man who I barely know, was my rock this evening. I know I could have done this without him, but I'm so glad I didn't.

As soon as we are in the car, Phillip breaks the silence.

"You didn't find what you were looking for, did you?" he asks gently.

I swallow down the lump that has risen in my throat. "No," I whisper. "I thought this would help me connect with my mum. But instead, it felt like strangers telling me stories about a stranger who *happened* to be my mum. They were nice people, but I don't know, I thought there would be this amazing bond that would form between us, and it didn't feel that way."

"I think the way you feel is normal," Phillip says slowly. "You waited so long for this meeting, you had time to visualize in your head how it would be, and it's hard for reality to match the picture you painted. It takes time to get to know people."

I find some peace with his words. "You're right. While I'm grateful I met them, and they told me things about my mum I never knew, I thought there would be some moment where I'd suddenly understand her. That I would feel this immense bond to her. That I would not only find the part of me that was missing, but I'd fill this hole that I feel inside of myself. But that didn't happen."

Oh, God, I've never said that out loud to anyone before. I turn my head away and gaze out at the row of houses we are parked in front of.

"Please forget I said that."

"No, I will not."

I turn to him, surprised by the forcefulness in his voice.

"Tell me why you feel as if you have a hole within you," Phillip presses.

"I don't know," I whisper back, barely able to say the words. "I always thought it was because of Anna, the mystery of her. That if I knew my mum, I'd somehow know myself and I'd have this complete sense of wholeness. The missing pieces would fill the hole. I know more about her now than I ever did, but I feel exactly the same inside."

Phillip takes in my words, and I can tell he's thinking before speaking.

"I don't think that's something your family can fill for you," he eventually says. "Blood families aren't people you choose to be in your life. I totally understand why you thought knowing all about Anna would change you, and knowing your family, and I'm sure on some levels it will. But anything you are feeling is missing inside of you is something you have to find for yourself."

I stare at him in amazement. His words resonate deep within my soul, and it's as if Phillip could see through my jumble of emotions and figure out that I need to find what is missing within myself.

Then my heart jumps inside my chest.

I always thought the key to finding myself would be Anna and the Brown family.

But now I'm not so sure.

Because I wonder if the key to myself is in different hands, in the hands of someone who sees me and understands me and isn't afraid to say what he's thinking. The person holding this key in his hands knows how to make me think and push me and will continue to do so until I figure this out.

And this key might be in the hands of Phillip Coventry.

78

Chapter Eight

I arise the next morning at my usual time, despite the fact that it's Saturday and I'm off. I fell into a deep sleep, exhausted and drained from my emotional meeting with the Brown family.

As soon as we returned to Montpelier Square, Phillip took me into the study, poured each of us a glass of brandy, and after I choked and spluttered and told him that it was the most vile thing I had ever drank in my life and my throat might very well be scarred by that varnish-like liquid, he laughed loudly and then told me to go to bed, because I might need to sleep off that one toxic gulp.

I found myself laughing with him and headed upstairs, only to remember we never talked about him avoiding me after I made that comment about Mooreton House. I resisted the urge to fly back downstairs to the study where I left Phillip and ask him to explain that to me. I'll have to ask him the next time I see him, which of course, who knows when that will be, as he doesn't live here.

But my heart tells me it will be soon.

Which is good and bad.

I sit up in bed and stretch my arms overhead, then turn my neck once to each side. The good? I can't wait to see him again.

I know I have a crush on him. These butterflies, the flittering of my heart, the way a smile lights on my face and warmth spreads through me whenever I think of him. He makes me feel alive in a way I've never felt with other men I've let into my life.

I frown. Which is bad.

Bad, because I've never had true love with anyone. Not that this is love—God, by no means is it that—but I have a crush on him and I care about him, and that could lead to something if Phillip ever reciprocates my feelings. But I remember how my Aunt Emily was back in California when she was heartbroken over love. The sobbing like she would never stop. Months of moping and moments where I'd catch her crying for no reason.

Then there's my father. Dad was so traumatized by losing Anna, he can't even talk about her. Why would I put myself through that? Isn't it safer to keep my heart protected and uninvolved? I'm happy for the most part—love would only complicate things.

Then there's really bad, part three.

Rose surely doesn't want her staff dating her brother. God, how unprofessional would that be? And let's say I did roll the dice like a betting fool and began to date Phillip and things ended badly? She'd fire me and fume that she should have hired a professional nanny in the first place.

I put my head in my hands and groan.

This whole road to figuring out the missing part of myself has become more complicated in ways I never dreamed possible.

I take a shower and change into some nicer clothing, which is something I enjoy doing on my days off. I slip into a short, black Sandro dress, which has ruffled straps and an asymmetrical hem with more ruffles. It's form-fitting and makes me feel rather feminine and flirty. I take some time to put my hair up in a triple-braided updo and slip in a pair of my Kendra Scott drop earrings. I apply my makeup, give myself a spritz of my perfume, and lastly, slip into my low-top white sneakers. I shrug into my white, cropped denim jacket, grab my purse, and head downstairs, ready for breakfast and then to go out and see item number one on my mum's favorite places list today.

I head down the multitude of stairs until I reach the level of the kitchen. To my utter shock, I see Phillip sitting at the kitchen island, a coffee mug parked in front of him, reading his phone with a scowl on his face.

"Phillip," I say. "I didn't expect to see you here this morning."

He immediately looks up the second he hears my voice. Then his eyes quickly skim over me, and goosebumps prickle my skin in response.

"I slept in the guest room. I had brandy, after all."

I smile. "Good point."

"You look beautiful," he says softly.

My stomach flutters with happiness. "Thank you." I move to the cupboard and retrieve a mug for myself, and then head over to the Nespresso machine. "Why are you so scowly this morning?"

"What? I'm not scowly."

I laugh. "You were scowling when I walked in. Why is that?"

"Georgina."

I select a pod and put it into the machine, and then hit the button to brew a cup of coffee. I turn around, curious at this.

"I don't know much about Georgina, except she's your youngest sister," I say.

"She's maddening," he says, the scowl returning. "But I don't want to talk about her now."

I bite my lip. I notice Phillip does this. When he starts to reveal something about himself—like that comment he made to me last night about his feelings, or his frustration with Georgina right now—he abruptly shifts gears to silent.

How many of his feelings are locked inside? I wonder. *And why is he so afraid to share them?*

I can tell by the scowl and the silence that now is not the right time to press him further on either item.

But I refuse to let him lock all these burdens within himself. He's so caring and compassionate with others, he deserves someone to give him a safe space to unburden his own worries.

After what he did for me yesterday—no, after what he has done for me since the moment he helped me up in the pasture—I vow to help him. As he's beginning to kick at the walls around my heart, I know I want to do this for him.

I will be your safe person, Phillip, I think fiercely.

Today, however, is not the day for that. I respect his wishes and open the fridge, grab some milk—ugh, do I miss half-and-half—and begin to doctor my coffee with it.

"What are your plans today?" Phillip asks, shoving his phone aside.

"I'm going to St. Paul's," I say, referring to the historical cathedral with the iconic dome that is a famous part of the London skyline. Satisfied that my coffee has enough milk, I put the carton back in the fridge and move so I'm standing across the island from Phillip.

"Your mum's favorite place," he says.

I nod.

He rubs his hand over his jaw, and I notice the golden stubble that is shading it now—rather thickly, too. Wow, that grew in fast, because it wasn't there when I had brandy with him last

82

night. I wonder what it feels like. Phillip looks very rugged and sexy right now, and my body responds accordingly. I suddenly feel warm and flushed.

Shit. I'm in serious trouble with this one.

"Let's put Anna's list aside for a moment," Phillip says slowly, as if he's testing the waters with the idea he's about to spring on me. "What is at the top of your list?"

I freeze. "My list?"

"Yes. If you could go anywhere in London today, where would you go?"

I pause and thoughtfully take a sip of my coffee. "Oh, there are so many things I want to see."

"Good, then give me three of them."

I raise an eyebrow. "That's rather demanding of you."

He raises one back. "Well, I am Lord Grace Viscount, you know. I can be an arse."

I laugh. "You could never, ever be an ass."

Phillip's smile fades. "Some people think I am."

My heart catches. My gut tells me this man in front of me—this wonderful, amazing, young man—has to be serious beyond his years. It's weighing on him. And I want to take this heaviness off that is blanketing him and bring the sparkle into his blue eyes again.

"Well, I don't think you are," I say defiantly. "Even if you do go about demanding lists from me without giving me the chance to take more than one sip of my coffee."

I see it. The hint of a smile comes back to his face.

"That's true. I should at least feed you before I go around making demands."

I laugh. "You don't have to feed me. And I can tell you three things I've always dreamed of seeing."

"Go on."

"Big Ben. I have to see that, of course," I say, ticking off a finger on my left hand. "Two, I want to take a tour of Buckingham Palace. Oh, and see the changing of the guard, but I kind of roll that into the second thing. Third—and this is more something you do—but I'm dying to ride one of those double decker buses with the open top, where they take you on a tour of London."

Now the appearance of a smirk appears on his ruggedly handsome face.

"Oh, don't smirk at me," I say playfully. "I'm a tourist. I have no shame in wanting to ride that bus."

"No, it ticks the tourist box," he says, taking a sip of his coffee. "By the way, I could probably get you a private tour of Buckingham Palace. I know both Christian and Xander."

My jaw practically swings on a hinge. He knows Christian and Xander.

As in Christian, the *Duke of Oxford,* and Prince Alexander of Wales—the future *king.*

Good God, Phillip might as well live on another planet when he drops things like this on me.

"I'm playing polo with them next month, as a matter of fact. Do you want me to ask?" Phillip asks.

Do I want him to ask?

It's all I can do not to hyperventilate at this point.

"Yes, if it's not a bother for you and you don't think they'd mind," I say, hardly believing I'm having this conversation.

"It's nothing. I'm a better polo player than either of them, so I'll use my position in future charity matches as leverage."

"Phillip! Don't you dare."

He grins wickedly at me. "I don't promise anything."

Secretly, I'm thrilled he wants to get me the ultimate tour of Buckingham Palace.

And knowing he's a better polo player than both the duke and the prince?

Freaking hot.

I clear my throat. "Okay. You're the native. What do you recommend I see?" I challenge.

"Borough Market," he says, not even thinking about it. "It's this brilliant food market with everything you could possibly want—and it's more than a thousand years old."

"Really?" I ask, intrigued by this.

"It's crammed full of stalls and shops with almost every food you can imagine," Phillip says. "You can get food to eat there, or you can get stuff to bring home and cook later. The smells are amazing."

"And this is one of your favorite places in London?" I ask, an idea coming to my mind.

He nods. "It makes me hungry just thinking about it."

"Well, you did say you should feed me this morning," I tell him.

Phillip's eyes widen in surprise. "What?"

"I've changed my mind. I think I want to go get breakfast at Borough Market. Do you want to come with me?" I ask.

He rakes a hand through his hair. "Hmm. I have stuff I should do today."

My stomach drops out. I overstepped a boundary. He went with me last night because he's kind and he cares about me—as a human being. Did my crush on him cause me to misread everything? And that comment he made last night, about not understanding his feelings—did I make that bigger than it was?

Regardless, I shouldn't have asked him to go with me to

Grace's house in the first place, but he did out of kindness.

Asking him to spend a Saturday with me at a food market is another.

That's asking far too much of him.

"I understand," I say, forcing a smile on my face. "Well, I'll let you get to it."

I quickly turn around, my smile fading the second my back is turned to him. I'm about to transfer my coffee to my portable tumbler so I can flee as soon as possible, but Phillip's voice stops me.

"I said there's work I *should* do. I didn't say I was doing it."

I turn around. "Pardon?"

"Screw my responsibilities for a morning. Let's go," Phillip says. "I checked the weather when I got up this morning—no rain in the forecast, so it's a perfect day to do it."

Elation fills every inch of me. I had no idea how badly I wanted him to say yes until I thought he was saying no.

"Let me grab some of Rose's shopping bags," Phillip says, getting off his stool. "We'll need those."

Rose.

"Phillip? Would Rose be okay with you escorting me to the market?" I ask, biting my lip.

He snorts. "Why wouldn't she be? Don't you dare say it's because you're the nanny."

"But I am."

"Am I your employer?"

"Well, no."

"Do I get to choose how I spend my free time?"

"Yes, but—"

"Did you or did you not ask me to go with you?" Phillip asks, interrupting me.

I blush furiously. "I did, but perhaps I shouldn't have, because I don't know what Rose would think."

"Quite frankly? What you do on your days off is none of her business. Also, she'd be thrilled I wasn't working, so she'd probably give you a raise for getting me out of the office."

He takes his coffee and dumps out what is remaining in the sink. He rinses his mug, sets it down, and then turns around and stares at me.

"So, does your offer still stand? Or are you taking it back?" he asks.

Phillip folds his arms across his chest and lifts an eyebrow at me in a challenging manner. I gulp as I notice how the fabric of his whisper blue T-shirt hugs his massive chest, and how powerful his forearms look. In a flash, heat once again rises within me.

"The offer still stands," I manage to say. "If Your Lord Grace Viscount wishes to go, that is."

He grins. The second he does, all my worries about crossing boundaries disappear. How can seeing this smile be wrong?

And how can this feeling of happiness I have inside be wrong, either?

"I do wish to go," Phillip says. "So, let me get those bags, and, if you're ready, we have a tube to catch."

* * *

I'm full of anticipation as we exit the underground at the London Bridge station and pop up right near the entrance to Borough Market. It's still early on this Saturday morning, and London is coming to life around us. The weather is mild, and the skies are partly cloudy, but no rain in the forecast, as Phillip said before we left.

It wouldn't matter if it did rain.

It could pour buckets, and I'd still consider it a perfect day.

Because Phillip has been smiling all morning.

I bask in the warmth of it. When he lets go, his sun is so strong that I can't help but feel warm in its presence. That's the best way to describe it.

"The coffee shop I like is at the far end. We can walk through the market and reach it when we come out the other side."

"Excellent. I can scope out what I want to have for breakfast."

He glances down at me. "Are you starving?"

I grin. "Famished."

"Coffee first, then I have something I'm going to suggest, but I want you to see it, and you can tell me if it's something you'd want to try."

"Ooh, a surprise."

"Yes. I am capable of one or two of those a year," he says dryly.

I laugh. "Oh, I think you are capable of surprises and adventures more than you give yourself credit for."

And if you'd allow yourself the freedom to let go more often, you would have so many wonderful adventures ahead of you, I think.

"Do you know the last time I did something like this? Completely unplanned?" Phillip asks as we make our way down the sidewalk.

Now I raise an eyebrow. "Last night, when you had dinner with me at the Browns'."

Phillip frowns, and I burst out laughing at the expression on his face.

"Right. Well, besides that, I mean."

"When we had our breakfast cookoff?" I supply helpfully.

Now Phillip shoots me a mock angry glare, and I can't help but grin from ear-to-ear in response.

"You're exasperating," he declares.

"No, but I seem to be the common denominator in your newly found spontaneous activities," I say.

Phillip stops walking, and I come to a stop, too.

"You are," he says quietly. "And for that, I'm grateful."

My heart races. People move around us, but I swear London has faded away in this moment. I stare up into his blue eyes, and I feel things I have never felt before, things that should make me terrified to be alone with him for fear of being too vulnerable.

But I'm not.

I feel comfortable with him. As if we can talk for hours and never be bored. Phillip challenges me, like he did today to let go of Anna's list—which had been part of my whole plan for coming to London—and not try to find her happiness in St. Paul's, but to find my *own* happiness instead.

Only Phillip could urge me to consider this choice. Something stirs in my heart, something so deep and powerful that my breath catches in my throat as the thought strikes the core of who I am.

Finding Anna wasn't the key to finding myself. I'm glad I know her better now and got to hear her stories from the sister who loved her. I know the parts of her that are parts of me, and that makes me happy.

But I realize now that Phillip is unlocking the key to the hole within me. The hole that has been created by the protective barriers I keep around my heart. While I'm happy with who I am—I don't believe you need a romantic partner to make your life complete—I now understand how letting someone get close to you can bring out new sides of yourself. I not only understand this, but I *feel* it.

Opening your heart is opening your senses, your experiences, your soul, and trusting another human being with it. It's allowing a different kind of joy, of happiness, and adding a richness to your experiences.

It always terrified me before to let someone this close to my heart. I couldn't see how any man could ever be worth this leap. Because I've seen people madly in love, only to be destroyed when people leave your life.

Yet as I stand here staring up into the bluest eyes I have ever seen, on this city street in London, I now know why people take these leaps.

It's for a chance at this great experience on earth called love.

Phillip clears his throat and inclines his head in the direction of the Borough Market entrance. "Shall we enter?"

We head inside, and it's as if I've entered another world. I gasp in delight upon sight of it. There are cafés and stalls and people everywhere, and it's only eight-thirty in the morning! My eyes are darting all around as we wind through it. I see fresh fish. A vast selection of breads. Wine shops. Thai street food. Glorious arrays of fresh produce. I inhale sausages sizzling on grills and see massive pans of paella cooking away. The choices here are utterly endless!

Samples are being passed out by vendors, and I swear, I have an immediate desire to try them all.

After breakfast, that is.

"Phillip, this is incredible," I say as we continue on our journey to coffee. I look up and see a train roll by overhead.

"I'm glad you think so," Phillip replies. "It's my favorite place to go on a Saturday morning."

"I can see why," I say as I hear a vendor call out something about oysters. "I would come here every Saturday to get my food for the week. And that's probably what I will do today."

We make it to the other side of the market, and there is a coffee shop that already has a line that goes out the door.

"Don't let the queue fool you," Phillip says, reading my mind. "It moves really fast."

"I don't mind waiting," I say as we cross the street.

Phillip smiles at me. "I didn't think you would. You have patience."

I giggle. "It's a key part of my job."

He chuckles. "I can't even imagine what my nieces and nephews put you through in a day."

"They're good kids," I say. "We're still getting to know each other, and I'm figuring out how to nurture each one so they can grow up to be amazing individuals."

Phillip studies me. "This is why you are so good for them. You don't see them as one older child and triplets. You see them as the unique personalities they all are."

I nod. "I do. It's going to take time to bond with them, but I'll do it. I know it takes a long time to get used to someone completely different who is going to be such an important person in their daily lives."

"You're becoming an important person in more than just their lives," he says, his voice low.

My heart leaps inside my chest. Is Phillip feeling all these same things that I am? That I'm becoming this person who can change his life, like he is already changing mine?

Suddenly, I blink, and my romantic thoughts and visions and ideas of walls tumbling down are smacked upside my head with a jarring dose of reality.

This is my employer's brother.

"What's wrong?" Phillip asks, as we move forward in line.

"Nothing," I reply, shaking my head.

"Please don't say that. I would think after everything we've been through this week, you can say anything to me now."

"My God," I gasp. "It was only a week ago yesterday that I met you. That seems like forever ago!"

"I know, I feel as if I've known you for so much longer," Phillip concurs. "I know the look you get in your eyes when your brain is tripped up on something, and you have it now. Is it something I said?"

I bite my lip. Do I dare say what is in my heart?

I gaze up at him again, the sun breaking through the clouds and shining down on his golden locks, the look of concern in the bluest eyes I have ever seen, and I decide I'm throwing it all to the wind now with what I'm about to say. I could be terminated. I could end up going back to California.

But I came here to find myself.

And while the journey is taking a completely different route than I ever could have imagined, I know I have to do it.

"Phillip," I say, my voice coming out in a nervous rush, "I like you. I think you know I do. But ... but you are my employer's brother. When I became a nanny, I vowed to conduct myself with morals and values, and I would never do anything to jeopardize my employer's trust."

Phillip's expression doesn't show any change, as if he's not surprised or affected by anything I said.

"We haven't crossed any lines," he says.

"Well, before any lines get crossed, I need to have a conversation with Rose and John," I say. "If you want to cross those lines, that is."

"McKenna, never doubt how badly I want to cross those lines

with you," he tells me, his deep voice low with desire.

My heart is fluttering wildly now, in rhythm with the butter-flies in my stomach.

"I have to talk to Rose first," I whisper.

"No, you don't," he says firmly.

I exhale. "Phillip, you know why I do."

"I do, and I'm telling you that you do not have to have that conversation with her. Because I already have. I had it with her last night."

Chapter Nine

I stare at Phillip in shock.

He's talked to Rose about us.

"What?" I gasp, barely able to get the word out.

"I will explain it after we get our coffee," Phillip says firmly.

Wait until we get our coffee? How am I supposed to wait with that sentence hanging out there for me to grapple with? My brain is torn in all directions. Phillip likes me enough to go straight to his sister to tell her he wants to date me? And what did Rose say—is she angry? Did Phillip ask permission, or much like that day in the pasture, did he come rolling in making decisions, and everyone acquiesced to the authority he wields? I'm half scared to death to think of her response. If she challenged it, did he get angry? Oh, God, this could go wrong in so many ways, I want to stop thinking about them.

I remain silent as we wait in line, my stomach churning the entire time. Phillip tries to engage me in light conversation, but I can't. I end up saying "yes" or "no" or "uh-huh," and he quickly gives up. Before long, we are walking out of the shop, coffees in hand, and Phillip remains silent as he leads me back through the market. I grow more anxious and exasperated with each step. I know I have endless patience with children, but when it comes to Phillip right now, I'm wearing thin. I have to know what was said. My future—my employment, my security in the UK, and dating him—all hang in the balance with whatever words are uttered from his lips. Yet here we are, walking through the market without a single word being said.

"Phillip, this is ridiculous," I snap at last. "We need to talk."

"We will, hold on," he says, leading me through the unfamiliar maze of vendors and foods. Now we are outside again, and the Southwark Cathedral appears in my vision. Phillip crosses the street, goes next to the cathedral, and takes the coffee from my hands. He sets both our drinks down next to the stone wall outside the church and looks at me.

"Now we can talk," he says, as the clouds roll over the sun, putting the sky in a dull gray around us.

"What did you say? What did she say?" I blurt out impatiently. "I'm dying here, Phillip!"

"I told Rose I had feelings for you," Phillip says bluntly.

My heart holds still. I don't dare breathe for fear this is all somehow a dream and I'll wake up from it. Because now that I know this is what is in his heart, mine is vulnerable to him.

And forever will be.

"You do?" I ask, my voice shaking.

"How can this be a surprise to you?" Phillip asks, his eyes growing wide in amazement. "Hasn't it been obvious since the day I came across you in that cow pasture?"

Oh, my God.

Phillip exhales and continues. "I liked you, but I wrestled with it. Not because of what Rose would say, I knew she'd be fine wit—"

"Wait, how did you know she'd be 'fine' with us dating?" I interrupt. "She's my *boss.* Doesn't she have concerns that you could distract me from doing my job? Or that I'd quit if we became involved and it didn't work out? Or that if you decided you didn't want to date me, she would have to fire me because you are her brother?"

A smirk appears on his full lips. I try to stay focused, but it's incredibly hard when I'm trying to imagine how it would feel to be kissed by that sensual mouth.

"Rose," he says, the smirk deepening, "doesn't have a leg to stand on. She's had one job in her life, and that was working as John's assistant. You can see how that ended up."

"Oh," I say as that picture sinks in.

"But I still wrestled with it. Partially because, yes, it could get awkward if we started seeing each other and it didn't work out. Yet my gut tells me that won't be the case. Not with you. Not with us. I've never had my gut scream at me like this in my life, to take this chance. I don't take chances. That's not who I am, nor is it the man I can ever be allowed to be."

I'm processing all his words with a mixture of pure hope and many questions. I'm about to ask what he means when he continues.

"I'm not the most exciting man in the world, I know that," Phillip says. "And you are so vibrant and full of life, and I don't know if I could ever make you happy. But despite what my head says, even when I tried to put distance between us after what happened at Mooreton House, I couldn't stop thinking about you."

My heart is thundering now. I gaze up at him, his light still bright despite the clouds, and feel nothing but happiness inside of me.

"Did you stay away because I said I couldn't imagine your life there?" I ask.

Phillip nods. "Yes."

"Well, considering I had just flashed a bunch of American tourists, I probably wasn't in the right frame of mind to consider all the pros and cons of living in a historic estate."

He smiles, and I do, too.

"But Rose is fine with this?" I ask, feeling a crease of worry form in my brow.

"You want to know her initial reaction?"

I wince. "Do I?"

He laughs, and I bask in the sound of it.

"She said, and this is a direct quote, 'Bloody hell, I would have hired her sooner if I'd have known this was going to happen.'"

"No!" I gasp, stunned.

"Rose," Phillip explains, "has wanted me to have my own life for a long time. She knows what kind of person you are. She's already seen how good you are with her children, and she thinks you could be good for me, too. McKenna, she knows you aren't going to ignore the kids to text me all day or quit in a rage if we date and break up. But I don't intend for that to happen."

My mouth falls open. "I can't believe this."

"I-I hope you aren't angry at me for speaking so candidly to Rose," he says.

"No, I'm not. Although, I will still have to speak to her myself. It's important that I reassure her no matter what happens, I will be there for the children. And for you," I say, gazing up at him with the feelings that are forming in my heart.

"There's a lot you don't know about my life," Phillip says firmly, a serious look taking over his face. "Things you might not want in someone you could potentially see as a boyfriend."

"Well, wouldn't the point of dating be to learn these things about each other?" I challenge. "I mean, you might see my other breast and decide you don't like them as a set."

He blinks at my comment, and I've succeeded in startling him. Then he throws his head back and roars with laughter, and I laugh, too.

"I have no doubt your other breast is equally as beautiful as the one you flashed me," he says dryly.

"I did not flash you, Your Lord Grace Viscount!"

He grins. Then he takes both my hands in his, and warmth spreads through my entire body the moment our hands are linked. His expression grows serious once again.

"Do you mean what you said? Are you willing to get to know the real me?" Phillip asks softly.

I squeeze his hands firmly in mine. "I am. I knew you were different from the moment I met you. I want you to open up to me about your life. I want to know everything about you. It doesn't scare me."

The clouds roll again, and this time, the sun breaks through brightly, basking both of us in warmth and light.

I gaze up into the blue eyes I trust, into the eyes of the man who is making me grab this moment. For so long, I've been afraid of letting anyone in. For so long, I thought a part of myself was missing. And it was, but not the part I thought.

It wasn't my mother's history that I needed.

Instead, all I needed was the bravery to open my heart to those around me.

To Phillip.

I'm standing on this edge now, where I can leap forward to Phillip and see where this path can go, or I can stay back where I'm safe and guarded.

He cups my face in his hands. My breath hitches as he leans closer to me. A light summer breeze carries his scent to me, and

I draw it in, the familiar scent of vanilla and spice and leather that lingers sensually on his skin.

"Will you take a chance on me?" he murmurs as he drops his lips right above mine. I shiver as I feel his breath on my skin. "Tell me, McKenna. Tell me you want me. Please let me hear you say it."

I'm shaking now. His whispers caress my lips, hot with need and desire. I feel the pads of his thumbs reverently tracing over my cheekbones and hear the heaviness of his breathing. I detect the urgency and need in his voice to have me tell him I do want this, to take this leap into the unknown with him, and only him.

"I do want you," I say, answering without fear. "More than I've ever wanted any man."

And the second those words are spoken, Phillip's lips find mine. His mouth, oh, his mouth is warm and soft and oh-so-gently lingering against mine in an innocent kiss. It's a mere touch of the lips, the briefest of moments, but enough to let loose a torrent of emotion and desire within me. Feelings I never dreamed could exist or be unleashed by a sweet kiss.

Phillip kisses me again, another chaste caress that has me yearning to open to him, my primal need to taste him and feel his tongue and explore a deeper, more intimate kiss burning within me. But I know this man. I know what a gentleman he is.

And Phillip would not kiss me like that in public. Not for our first kiss.

His lips linger over mine, a groan of desire escaping his throat, and then he lifts his head. I stare up at him, spellbound that my lips have touched his in the sweetest kiss I have ever known.

"Thank you," he murmurs, caressing my face in his huge hands. "Thank you for giving me a chance. And a kiss," he adds, grinning sexily at me.

I tentatively reach up to place my hands on his chest. I can feel his heart pounding underneath his shirt as his arms now move around my waist, holding me to him. My heart pounds again, but this time, from how right this feels. How good it is to be in Phillip's arms, to have him gaze down upon me with such affection in his eyes.

"I will give you more kisses if you should desire them, Your Lord Grace Viscount," I tease.

His smile deepens. "God, I certainly hope so. It would be disappointing if we ended it there."

I laugh. "I agree."

Phillip draws me into his chest, his hand skimming my back, and I close my eyes and breathe him in, desperately wanting to keep this moment forever in my head. I feel his lips brush the top of my head, and I sigh deeply in happiness.

"Are you starving?" Phillip asks, his deep voice breaking the silence.

I step back so I can look up at him. "Yes."

Phillip bends down and retrieves my drink. "Here's your coffee," he says.

"Thank you," I reply, taking a sip of my flat white. "Oh! This is delicious!"

"It is good, isn't it?" Phillip says, pausing to take a drink of his own latte.

"It's smooth and creamy." I take another sip.

"Now," Phillip says, "we need something to go with it."

"Ooh, what are we getting?"

"The most amazing donuts you have ever had in your life," Phillip tells me.

I giggle. "You are quite confident that I am going to not only like these, but love them," I say.

"I am. After all, I was pretty confident you were going to let me kiss you."

"What?" I shriek, laughing. "You asked me!"

"Well, that's the polite thing to do. I knew you wouldn't be immune to my charms," he teases.

"Liar."

"You're right. I was *hoping* you'd say yes." Phillip reaches for my free hand and entwines it with his. "And luckily, you did say yes." He leans over and drops a delicious kiss on my lips, causing my heart to sing with happiness once again.

We cross the street, and after walking for a short bit, I find myself back in the market and moving toward a stall filled with donuts.

"Wait until you see these," Phillip says. "They are stuffed with the most brilliant fillings."

As soon as we approach, I'm given the task of trying to select one of the luscious donuts in front of me. I see donuts filled with vanilla cream and chocolate. Jelly filled. Then I pause, staring down at one filled with Nutella custard.

"Ooh," I say to Phillip. "I have to have that Nutella one."

"What else?" he asks.

"Hmm." I study the rest of the flavors. "Vanilla. What about you?"

"They have my favorite today," Phillip says. "Strawberries and cream. I love that combination."

"Oh, I bet that's good. The strawberries I had last weekend were delicious."

"I might be persuaded to share it with you," Phillip says, arching an eyebrow at me.

I laugh. "Oh, is that so?"

"One kiss for each bite sounds like an even exchange. But then

I'd be handing you the whole donut with that kind of exchange rate."

Swoon.

We end up buying four of them, adding a blueberry-jam filled one for good measure.

"We can walk down to the Thames and eat them with a view, if you like," Phillip suggests.

"Oh, can we please?" I ask excitedly. "That sounds like a quintessential London experience, having donuts with a famous view."

"Not quintessential," Phillip says. "It's your experience. *Your* London."

My heart soars with his words. I'm reminded by this amazing man that while I came to discover a part of my past, there is no reason why I can't create memories of my own choosing. That I can experience London with my own eyes.

And with Phillip by my side.

Phillip leads me back to the Thames, and we find a spot where we can sit. A gentle breeze rolls across us, and I watch as a boat moves past us, leaving rippling waves in its wake.

"Moment of truth," Phillip says, opening the box and setting it between us. "I promised you these will be the best donuts you have ever had. Now I need to hear what you think."

I inhale the heavenly scent of baked goods and sugar and nearly swoon from that alone.

"They even smell fantastic," I say, picking up my Nutella donut. I laugh as I look at it. "I don't even know how I'm going to eat this without making an incredible mess!"

Phillip grins. "You don't worry about the mess. You take a bite and enjoy it, that's what you do."

"Okay," I say gamely. "I'm going in."

I take a bite. My mouth is filled with such goodness, I could nearly cry with food joy. The donut is light and airy and covered in sugar. And the Nutella custard! My God, can such bliss exist within a donut? I feel sugar all over my lips and custard on my mouth, and I can't help but laugh as soon as I swallow my bite.

"I have this donut all over me," I say, grinning happily.

Phillip chuckles and picks up a napkin, and to my surprise, he leans over and gently blots my lips for me. The gesture is kind and protective—the traits I've already come to admire so strongly in him are demonstrated in this one simple move.

"There. Carry on," Phillip says.

I giggle. "Oh, I will, this is too good not to."

Phillip picks up his strawberries-and-cream donut and takes a bite, and I laugh as the cream ends up on the tip of his nose. Now it's my turn to take care of him, and I quickly dab it away with a napkin, which makes him chuckle.

"I look like one of the kids, I'm sure," he jokes.

I smile warmly at him. "Don't worry. I have wipes in my purse if you get out of control."

Phillip offers me a bite of his donut, and I let him feed it to me, his fingertips lightly touching my lower lip as he does. Heat flickers through me from that touch, and for a moment, I can't think of the donut, but of him. Of how I want to kiss him again.

"I believe I owe you a kiss for that," I say after I finish my bite.

"Yes, you do."

I lean in, and my lips meet his, tasting of sugar and cream and berries, and I sigh blissfully against his mouth.

"Mm," I say, lifting my head. "Your Lord Grace Viscount, your kisses are divine."

Phillip's eyes shine brightly at me. "That's not the donuts

talking, is it?"

"No, I assure you, it's not."

Phillip clears his throat. "What if I were to tell you I already know I'm not content with today?"

"What do you mean?"

"I know we're going to have this day at the market, but that's not enough for me. Normally, I follow Georgina around Mayfair on Saturday nights. I skipped last weekend, and I think I need to skip tonight, too."

I furrow my brow as an understanding hits me. "Phillip! Is that why you go to nightclubs? To keep an eye on your sister?"

It all makes sense now. Why he looks so miserable whenever he's snapped leaving them. The scowl on his face, why he's never pictured with women or getting stumbling drunk.

Phillip isn't there because he wants to be.

He's there out of duty.

I stare at him, and before my eyes, the serious expression returns to his face. He shifts his gaze out to the River Thames, and he remains silent for a moment.

"Yes," he finally says, his voice low. "Georgina is wild. She's partying until the clubs close. I've kept her out of more scandals than you can even count by stepping in or taking her home when she drinks too much. She's making all kinds of money with her social media influencing and modeling gigs, but she's spending it at an obscene rate, too. I manage her bills, and my father still has to cover at the end of the month. She insists on dropping out of uni, which I would be fine with if she proved to be an adult and was managing her money, but she's not. And I'm about to lose my bloody mind dealing with it."

My stomach sinks in despair. I know there are always differences between siblings, and I see that Phillip is obviously the responsible one, but good God, why is this on his shoulders? Why are his parents in Italy if Georgina is a problem? Why aren't they here being the parents?

Or why don't they let Georgina suffer the consequences of her actions and learn from them? She's not Layla's age.

She's nineteen.

And I wonder if she has ever been held accountable for anything in her life.

"Phillip," I say carefully, putting my hand on his and squeezing it, "that is not your responsibility to bear. You can't follow Georgina around the rest of her life saving her. She is going to have to learn to rely on herself, not you coming to bail her out whenever she gets herself in a mess."

He keeps his eyes straight ahead. "It's not that simple, McKenna. There are things you don't know. Promises I—"

Phillip abruptly stops speaking. He removes his hand from mine and laughs ruefully. "This is why I stayed away from you this week. This right here. You are so full of light and happiness, and I'm like the dark cloud rolling over you with these responsibilities, ones you don't even know about. Besides the estates and trying to keep them making money. Besides Georgina."

"Phillip," I say, my tone firm, "look at me."

He turns, and I see dismay in those beautiful eyes.

"I accept you as you are. We all have dark clouds. You have helped me step through mine, and I will help you step through yours if you will let me. I'm not afraid of that. I don't see you as a dark cloud, but as my light. My sun. Don't you see that? We have so much more to discover about each other, sunshine and rain, but I never expected all sunny days. Nor do I want them, because that's not a genuine life."

Phillip draws in a breath of air. "How are you real?" he whispers. "How did you find your way to me?"

The sun breaks through the clouds again, and as it does, an epiphany rockets through me, one so powerful, I would fall to my knees if I were standing.

"Anna," I whisper, my heartbeat quickening. "Anna brought me to you, don't you see that?"

His eyes search mine, and I feel my own eyes grow wet with tears.

"You're right," he says, his expression going soft. Phillip cups my face in his hands, not caring about the sugar stickiness on his fingers, and draws me to him, placing a gentle kiss upon my lips and moving back so he can gaze down at me. "She did. And I'm not wasting another moment now that she's brought me to you."

"What do you mean?" I ask, staring up into his face.

"Tonight starts a new chapter for me. I'm not going to a nightclub. I'm going out. With you. I'm taking you out for dinner and drinks, and we're going to talk for hours, and then I'm going to kiss you until your lips are numb, that's what I'm going to do. I'm living for me now. For us. If you will go out with me, that is."

Happy tears fill my eyes. "After I talk to Rose, I will happily go to dinner with you. And drink with you. And kiss you until an obscene hour in the morning."

The smile returns to his eyes. And as he kisses me, I say a little thank you to the heavens above. To Anna.

To my mum.

For knowing exactly what I needed and for putting me in Phillip's path.

I know deep in my bones our date tonight will only confirm

that my mum does indeed know what I need.

And that's Phillip Coventry.

Chapter Ten

After a glorious morning of shopping at the market—and bags full of fresh produce, meats, and cheeses for the week ahead—Phillip and I find ourselves back at Montpelier Square. As soon as we step inside, I hear cartoons blaring from the TV in the kitchen, the sound of a pan crashing into a sink, the scent of something burning, a shriek of "noooooooooo!" and then John's rumbling voice telling everyone to wait their turn "while Daddy puts out the fire."

And then the fire alarms go off.

Phillip cocks an eyebrow at me. "Sounds like lunch when you aren't running it."

I hurry into the kitchen to find a sheet pan smoking in the sink and Rose flicking a towel about in the air to try and dissipate the smoke. Louis has his hands over his ears, Byron looks cross, and Pippa keeps asking if the chicken nuggets are ruined.

Layla turns to Louis. "The house is going to burn down."

Louis's lip trembles. "The house is not going to burn down!"

"What is going on?" Phillip asks, his voice breaking through the chaos.

"Phillip will save us!" Pippa cries.

John rolls his eyes. "Phillip doesn't need to save anyone."

"Oh, hello, it looks like you two went shopping this morning," Rose yells over the blaring alarm.

Phillip puts the bags down on the island and strides over to the oven, turning on the vent fan, which didn't seem to occur to either John or Rose.

"What happened?" Phillip asks.

"Daddy burnt our nuggets, and now we're going to starve," Layla says dramatically.

"Nobody is going to starve," John declares, his voice exasperated. "Just had the oven temperature wrong."

"He never reads directions," Rose says. "Hence, we have black nuggets."

John shoots her a look, and I bite the inside of my cheek to keep from laughing.

"So, will you all be heading to a pub for lunch?" Phillip asks.

"Yes, let's go to the pub," Pippa says. "I'm hungry!"

"I suppose we are," John says. "Would you and McKenna like to join us?"

Phillip glances at me and then back at them. "No, thank you. I think we're both still full from breakfast and tasting everything in the market."

I grin. That's no lie. After breakfast, we strolled through every nook and cranny of the market. I happily accepted every sample that was given to me, so needless to say, I'm still stuffed.

"Very well. Kids, get your shoes on," John calls out.

They all go scrambling toward the front door, where their shoes are lined up. As soon as they are out of earshot, I turn to Rose and John.

"May I have a word with you before you go?" I ask. Then I glance at Phillip. "Privately?"

"Of course," John says.

Phillip nods, as he knows what I need to say. "I'll go supervise the shoes."

Rose turns off the TV, and once the fire alarm is off, I nervously clear my throat.

"I know Phillip had a conversation with you about me," I say.

To my surprise, both Rose and John smile in response.

"We couldn't be more delighted," Rose says. "I saw that spark he had for you on the day you met. He's never had that for anyone."

My heart soars with this insider information, but I keep myself focused on what I have to say.

"I care about Phillip, too," I say. "But I want you to know that was never by design or who he was. It's the man he is. I could list all the attributes I like about Phillip, but I'm afraid the children will pass out in hunger while they wait."

John smiles at me. "I felt the same way about Rose. When she was assigned to be my assistant, I knew I was in trouble. That I shouldn't be involved with her, but my heart knew she was the one, and I wasn't going to deny myself happiness."

Rose beams from his words, and then she leans over and kisses his cheek affectionately.

"I want to assure you that in no way will this interfere with my work," I say firmly. "You are being incredibly understanding, being that you barely know me, but when I'm working, I'm *working*. And if things don't work out between Phillip and myself, I plan to handle it like an adult and continue working as your nanny, as long as you allow me to."

"McKenna, your previous employers all raved about you when I checked your references," Rose said. "All of them said how professional you were. How much their children loved you. All of them said they had never had a nanny like you since. I have

110

no doubt that whatever happens with you and Phillip, you can be adults about it. Though my hope is that you can take some of the adult out of Phillip."

"I hope so, too," I say quietly.

"We support this," John says, nodding. "For both of you."

"Thank you," I reply.

"Mummy!" Layla yells, coming back into the kitchen. "We're ready!"

Soon, the Palmerstons are out the door, and I find myself alone with Phillip in the kitchen. He slides his arms around my waist and gazes down at me, affection burning bright in his blue eyes.

"Now I'm going to leave you," he murmurs.

"You are?" I ask.

"I have to get ready for our date tonight," he says, dropping another innocent kiss on my lips.

It's all I can do not to grab his face and seriously kiss the life out of him. But I wait too long, and Phillip rises before my lips can take action.

I clear my throat. "How should I dress? Where exactly are we going for dinner?"

Phillip grins broadly at me, making my body weak. "You can wear jeans. The restaurant is a surprise, however."

I smile happily. "I love surprises."

"Good, I'll make a note of that," he murmurs, caressing my face in his hands. He drops a kiss on my forehead, then on my nose, and finally on my lips. "Now I'm off. I have things to do before this evening. I'll come round at six for you."

"Okay, I'll be ready," I say. Then I lift an eyebrow. "That's early, isn't it?"

"There's a reason for that," Phillip says mysteriously.

Then, before I can get another word out of him, he leaves me in the kitchen with no clue as to where we are going.

I wrap my arms around myself and grin broadly. I'm going on a date with Phillip, and he could take me out for a pint and a slice of pizza, and I'd be happy. As long as I'm with him, that's all that matters.

With that thought in my head, I happily go about putting away my groceries—but think of Phillip the entire time. I can't wait to see him tonight.

And I'll be counting down the minutes until six this evening.

* * *

I walk down the steps, excitement running through me as I do. Phillip just texted me that he was in the foyer, at the bottom of the stairs.

Waiting for me.

I can't keep the smile off my face. I can't wait to be with him, to continue our conversation, and oh, I *cannot* wait to receive a full kiss from him at some point during the night.

I reach the top of the final flight of stairs, and when I stand there, I see Phillip waiting at the bottom of the stairs for me. My mouth parts upon sight of him, as he's dressed in dark-washed jeans and a white dress shirt, with a navy blazer thrown over the top.

Oh, my, he's beyond handsome this evening, looking so polished with that fine blazer on. That's something a *man* would do, taking the effort to put on a blazer for a date. He wanted to be sharp for me this evening, which makes my heart skip a beat.

His eyes move over me, taking in the one-shoulder black top and skinny jeans I'm wearing. Phillip's eyes move all the way down to my strappy black heels and slowly back up to my face, appraising every inch of me.

"My God," he says, exhaling loudly as I descend the stairs. "You look beautiful this evening."

I blush happily from his compliment. "Thank you," I say as I reach the bottom step.

He stares down into my face. "Gorgeous," he murmurs softly as he takes my hands in his. "You are the most gorgeous woman I have ever seen."

I smile up at him. "You never dreamed how nicely I'd clean up when you found me flat on my back in that cow pasture."

A devilish smile passes over his sexy mouth. "Oh, I did imagine you'd clean up very nicely."

Now I'm really blushing, and he laughs loudly.

"But I thought you were beautiful even then," Phillip says. "Now, my beautiful lady, are you ready to go?"

I nod eagerly. "Yes. I can't wait to see where we're going tonight."

Soon we're off, and instead of taking the tube where we need to go, Phillip escorts me to a black cab that is waiting for us.

"I didn't want you to have to walk in heels," he explains.

I decide that if you were to look up a word in the dictionary at this moment to describe Phillip, *perfect* is the only thing that works.

"Thank you," I say, sliding into the backseat. Phillip follows, and he sits close to me, his massive leg brushing against mine. My body temperature instantly shoots up the second we touch.

"Are you ready for drinks and dinner?" Phillip asks, reaching for my hand again.

"I know you're an older soul, but I never pictured you wanting to grab the early bird," I say, teasing him.

A scowl immediately crosses his face, and it's all I can do not to grab him and kiss him.

"I'm not an old soul," he protests. "Not by choice, anyway."

My smile fades. I don't want him to feel this way. I want to give him the gift of gleeful abandon. To not feel the weight of his responsibilities, both those I know of and the ones I have yet to learn. Phillip deserves to live for himself and not for everyone around him.

And I vow, right here as I sit beside him, that I'm going to help him do that.

"What's the early bird?" he suddenly asks.

"It must be an American thing. It's when you go out for an unusually early dinner. It's often favored by senior citizens."

His scowl deepens. I burst out laughing.

"I'm only teasing you, Lord Grace Viscount."

I see him try to repress a smile. "There's a reason we're going to this early bird."

"Ooh! Are we doing something like a movie afterward?" I ask, intrigued.

The scowl turns into a smirk. "Please, would I do anything that awfully cliché for a first date with you?"

"The theater?"

"No."

"A concert?"

Phillip grins. "No. And I'm not going to tell you."

I continue to guess as we head into London, but I run out of ideas, and we talk about other things. We hit traffic, and now I understand why Phillip wanted to leave early. We creep our way along, and I still can't help but stare at the cultural icons that are within my view from the cab window. As we pass by Trafalgar Square, I keep my eyes peeled at the vibrant landmark, still

114

full of people even at this early evening hour. I see the famous Nelson's Column, of course, and the fountains and the steps leading up to the National Gallery. I feel a ripple of excitement. There is so much in London to explore. I glance back at Phillip, who is looking out the window closest to him, wrapped up in his own thoughts.

Thanks to this incredible man, I now want to not only see Anna's London, but my own London, too.

My heart flutters inside my chest. There's another London I want to see, one that is speaking loudly to me as I ride through this city with Phillip at my side.

I want a London with Phillip.

I want a London that is built on our collective shared experiences. A London that is filled with our favorite restaurants and markets and sporting events and museums and views from historic sites as the sun sets. I want memories of us looking at art and me cheering on his favorite soccer team and us bickering over the best pizza in the city.

Suddenly, a memory floods my brain. Something Grace said to me jolts my soul. When we were at dinner, eating some of my mum's favorite things, she spoke about my parents and how Anna knew early on my dad was her soul mate. Grace said she told Anna she was crazy at the time, that nobody can know within a few dates if someone is The One, but Anna insisted she knew it. She knew it with every fiber of her being, with every breath she took, that my dad was the man she would marry. That he had captured her heart, and he would always have it.

My pulse quickens as Anna's thoughts merge with my own. I can see falling in love with this man next to me. I can see it happening over dates and kisses as we open up to each other. I can imagine making love to him and feeling that kind of powerful intimacy that is tied with emotions—something I have never known in previous sexual experiences. I can see it with such precision and clarity, the wind is nearly knocked from me.

But not out of fear, like I always thought I would feel.

I'm breathless with excitement and happiness for a future that could be *mine.*

The cab pulls over near the River Thames, and we get out of the car. The city is alive around us on this Saturday night, and while the clouds are now blanketing the city and coloring it a shade of gray, I feel nothing but sunshine.

Thanks to the man who is holding my hand.

"I can't wait to see what you have planned," I say excitedly.

"You're going to love it." Phillip lifts his free hand and points toward a double-decker bus with a glass top.

"See that bus?" he asks.

"Yes."

"The top floor of the bus is a restaurant. You can get a panoramic view of London while you eat."

I stop walking. Phillip continues speaking.

"It's a four-course meal we'll be having, with wine pairings," he says. "And for the next three hours, you will have your bus tour of London. The bus is going to pass back and forth over the Thames and by all the key landmarks, pausing at each one so you can get amazing pictures."

Tears fill my eyes. Nobody has ever given me a gift like this. Phillip is giving me the top item on my London wish list tonight, but he's made it a thousand times better than anything I ever could have dreamed of.

I respond by moving in front of him, so I can face him, and throwing myself into his muscular arms, hugging him tightly.

"I'm going to ugly cry," I choke out.

"No, no, as Viscount Brookstone, I *forbid* you to do that," he teases.

I laugh and step back from him. I refrain from crying, but Phillip's face is blurry though my unshed tears.

"This is perfect," I manage to say over the lump in my throat. "Thank you."

"We're early. So we can sit down, and you can get rid of those tears that I am certainly not worthy of," Phillip says dryly.

"You," I say, my voice thick, "are worth every single one of these happy tears."

We sit on a bench near the bus stop, which overlooks the Thames. We talk about all the things we are going to see on the tour, and how many of them Phillip has actually seen, and we recognize ones that are on Anna's list, too. But what I love the most is that Phillip is smiling and chuckling at things I say. His arm is resting around the tops of my shoulders, and while it's the first time he has done that, it feels so natural and comfortable, it might as well be the hundredth time he's put his arm around me.

I'm so excited for the tour, I keep picking up his wrist and checking his watch.

"It's almost seven, we can go back across the street," I say eagerly.

Phillip grins. "I think I need to get you a watch. Although maybe I shouldn't, if it gives you a reason to grab me."

"Grab you?" I cry, laughing as we stand up. "I'm grabbing you as much as I flashed you on purpose."

"A man can dream, can't he?" Phillip says, raising his eyebrows suggestively at me.

As I get a view of his tight bum in his jeans, I decide when the time is right, I'll grab that instead of his wrist and let him know his dreams can be a reality.

Along with mine, I think mischievously.

We cross back over toward the bus and board it. We then take the stairs to the top deck. I'm so excited, I'm nearly bouncing on my toes as I see London all around me from the glass ceiling of the bus.

We are shown to a table for two, and as soon as we are seated, a sharply dressed server appears with champagne. As soon as he leaves, Phillip raises his champagne glass to me.

"Cheers," he says.

"Cheers," I say, tapping my glass against his.

Soon, we are off, and the experience is nothing short of magical. We pass by the great icons of London, and thanks to the bus, we get to see them from angles I never dreamed of. We're served course after course of fine food and wines. Phillip and I talk about each landmark, and I love hearing his personal connections to each one, whether it was a school trip visit or something from his family's ancestry—it's astounding to think of how deep his family roots are in this land.

When we come to St. Paul's Cathedral, I grow silent, thinking of Anna and seeing why she thought it was so breathtaking. I take pictures, and Phillip does, too, and soon I put my phone down and stare up at the famed dome that is such a focal point in the London skyline. This was her favorite place. Goosebumps prickle my skin as I feel more connected to her than I ever have.

Phillip reaches across the table for my hand, squeezing it gently.

I look back at him through the tears in my eyes. Anna is here in this moment. I will never know her the way I want, but she is with me. She guided me here. To this city, to this man, and now to this moment where he's looking at me so tenderly and with so much concern, my heart can barely process it.

"She's here, Phillip," I say, my voice unsteady.

"I know she is," Phillip says. "I feel her, too."

Our journey continues, and driving over the Tower Bridge is one of the coolest things I've ever done. I get some amazing photos of Phillip underneath the Tower Bridge, and he takes some of me, too. We wave at people on other buses, declaring that taking a bus this way—with wine—is our new and only way of taking a bus.

By the time the tour is over, London has fallen dark and the city lights shimmer all around us. I'm a bit buzzed from the wine and drunk with happiness from the entire experience. We exit the bus into the night, and Phillip takes my hand in his. To my surprise, he leads me back across the street, so we're standing in front of the River Thames, under a streetlamp. I shiver, as the temperature has dropped, and Phillip lets go of my hands and begins to remove his blazer.

"Here," he says, gently draping it over my shoulders. "I won't have you cold."

I gaze up at him. The butterflies go crazy in my stomach, and my heart begins to race.

"I have held back from kissing you for so long," he murmurs, cradling my face in his hands. "I don't know if I can wait until we get back to my flat to do it."

All of my nerves leap. My gaze drops to his mouth, and I yearn for those lips to find mine, right here, right now.

Phillip dips his head. I move my hands around his back, the fine fabric of his dress shirt sliding underneath my fingertips.

"Phillip," I whisper, my breath rushing across his lips. "Kiss me."

His mouth grazes mine, but suddenly, his phone blares in his blazer pocket, with a ringtone I have never heard from it before.

Phillip leaps back, his eyes blazing in fury in response to the sound. "Damn it!"

I reach inside the pocket and pull out the phone. The screen is facing me, and I see one name across it.

Georgina.

"Do you need to take this?" I ask, extending his phone to him.

He angrily rakes his hands through his hair. "I wanted one night. One bloody night, is that too much to ask for?"

My sunshine is gone. Phillip's eyes are now a thunderstorm of anger and worry, and I know I can't make this disappear now.

"I'm okay, you can take it," I encourage.

"It's not okay. It's not okay for you," he says, his voice rumbling with fury. Phillip takes the phone and abruptly answers it. "This better be an emergency, Georgina."

I bite my lip and draw Phillip's blazer a bit closer to me. I watch his face furrow as he listens, then he goes white in front of my eyes. My chest draws tight. Something is very wrong, and it's obviously fallen at Phillip's feet to fix it.

"Jesus Christ," he sputters. "No ... no, I'll sort it out. Where are you?" He laughs bitterly. "Of course, you are ... No, I'll be right there. ... It will take me fifteen minutes or so."

Then he hangs up. Phillip begins pacing in front of me, his hands to his head, and he looks tortured by what he was told on that phone call.

"Phillip," I say, putting my hand on his arm and bringing him to a stop, "talk to me."

My words cause him to jerk his head toward me, and I've never seen such sadness on his face as I do right now.

"I should have known I couldn't have done this," he says, his voice unsteady.

I grow colder from his expression. Alarm bells go off in my head. "What?"

He whirls around and puts his hands on my shoulders. "I never should have gotten involved with you."

I gasp. The blood drains from my face. I stare at him, blinking, not making sense of this.

"McKenna, you deserve better than this!" he practically shouts. "I have to manage this shitshow that is my family, and you shouldn't be dragged into this. I can't even have a night to myself on a weekend, how messed up is that? Do you know what that call was about? Do you? My sister sent bloody nudes to an ex-boyfriend in a fit of jealousy, and now he's sharing them all over the internet. Do you know what this means for her emotional state? For our family? For our name, which is how I manage to keep the estates paid for and afloat? She's drunk—I need to collect her and take her home. I'll probably have to call solicitors to sort out this mess. Then I have to decide if I should tell my father and if he'll even understand what I'm saying. Then I have the normal things to figure out how, like how we're going to get chairs refinished in gilt and tapestries fixed and what to sell so we can do it so we're still a top tour. But that's a whole other issue. I promised to keep Georgina in line, and I *failed* tonight. You deserve the world, and none of this, not a man who is running from one crisis to the next, and I was a selfish bastard to think I could have you in my life at the same time."

My head is spinning. He doesn't know what he's saying—the words are pouring out of him like a dam of frustration that has finally, after all this time, erupted under the strain of his responsibilities.

And I'm about to be a casualty of it if I can't stop him.

"I will go with you," I say firmly. "You need me."

"No!" Phillip roars. "I can't need you, I can't, because it will gut me when you realize you don't want to live like this."

"Don't I get to decide that?" I cry.

"No, you don't. Not when you deserve better than me. You don't want to live in the country, you don't want a home that is open to the world, you don't deserve a boyfriend who has to act like he's bloody fifty. You deserve more, and you are going to have it. But you can't have it with me."

Phillip walks to the sidewalk, and to my horror, throws up his hand to hail a black cab.

"What are you doing?" I cry, trailing him.

"I'm getting a cab to take you home," he says flatly.

"You are not," I say, angrily jerking his hand down. "I'm not going anywhere without you."

"You don't have a choice," Phillip replies, his voice shaking. "You need to pretend we never happened."

I feel as if a knife has been launched into my heart.

Pretend we never happened.

I finally let down my walls. I let Phillip in, something I've been terrified to do my entire life, and now he's ending it before we even began.

But it's too late for me.

Because he already has a piece of my heart.

"I trusted you," I blurt out, my voice thick with unshed tears. "I never trusted anyone, and I thought you were the one man I could."

Phillip looks stricken by my words. "Please, don't. This is hard enough as it is."

"You are the one who is making it hard!" I scream at him, not caring that we have become a sideshow on the street. "I was so afraid of this. That I would let someone in, and he would break my heart. I was falling for you, Phillip. You had my heart in your hands, and you threw it away. You shattered it. You're an idiot. An idiot! Because none of the things you told me scare me, not one of them. Things happen in life that are messy. I'm living proof of how heartbreaking and messy life can be, but my father has shown me resilience. That if you believe in love, you can fight for things and get through things. He is the bravest man I know, learning to love again. But you will never have love like that, because you don't think you're worth it. And that's the biggest tragedy of all."

Now I throw my hand up, as I need to get away from him. I'm falling apart inside—it's only a matter of seconds before I go to pieces right in front of him.

"McKenna, wait," he pleads. "Not like this."

A black cab pulls right up to me, and I've never been more grateful to see one in all my life. I jerk open the door, but Phillip puts his hand on it to stop me.

"No, I won't let you go," he says, his voice commanding.

"You already did," I tell him, my voice shaking with pure anger. I gaze into his eyes, which are full of anguish. I can barely see him through my tears now, but I refuse to ugly cry in front of him. "You have broken my heart. You have taken control of everyone around you, and the last person I ever expected you to try and control was me. But you did. You made this decision for me, and I have no choice in it, do I? How dare you decide what is best for my heart. This is the one area you don't have to worry about or manage, don't you see that?"

Phillip's hand falls from the cab door. He lurches backward, as if I've just punched him in the stomach.

"Well, I've learned my lesson. I opened my heart to you, and this is the price I have to pay. I'm devastated. And I will never, *ever,* trust you with it again."

I jerk the door closed. I tell the driver the address to Montpelier Square. I purposely don't look back at Phillip as the car drives off into the night.

Then I can smell him.

I look down, and I still have his blazer on. My heart breaks all over again with this reminder of Phillip. The scent of his cologne wraps around me like a blanket, holding me in a way Phillip never will again.

And with that thought, I burst into tears.

Chapter Eleven

I sit on my window ledge and watch as the sun begins to come up on another London day, streaks of orange and pink filling the sky.

Except there is no sun in my world.

Because the man who became my sun—my warmth, my light—is gone.

I close my eyes as they refill with new tears. As soon as I got home last night, I cried like I remembered watching Emily cry all those years ago. I cried for what my heart knew we could have been. Phillip was different. *We* were different. I didn't need to kiss him deeply or make love to him or even be in love with him to know what we were going to be.

Like Anna, I knew. Within a week of knowing him, I knew he was the man I wanted to be with. To fall madly in love with, to surrender my entire heart to.

And now it's gone.

This is the pain I wanted to avoid. This hole in my heart, this sick feeling of never being with Phillip ever again—this is why I had protected myself for so long.

I bite my lip. But I know that's a lie.

I protected myself until the right man came along. And then

those barriers didn't matter anymore. Even though he's the brother of my employer, I didn't care. The walls were coming down for a reason.

Because Phillip was the right man to lower them for.

Yet he wants to pretend we never happened.

Fresh anguish fills me. How can he want that? How can Phillip think this is best for me?

My phone rings.

Hope fills my heart as I rush over to it on the nightstand. But I'm crestfallen when I see it's my mom wanting a Connectivity Video Connect.

I swallow hard. I don't want to talk to anyone right now, yet I need my mom. And that need wins out as I accept the call.

"Hey! I—McKenna, what's wrong?" Mom quickly asks, her face instantly one of concern.

"Oh, Mom," I cry, falling apart all over again. "Mom, I-I—"

The ugly crying begins. Mom knows how to handle this, and she soothes me the best she can through a video call. When I finally pull myself together, I tell her the whole story. Everything from how Phillip and I met to the most romantic night of my life to him shoving me away. She listens carefully, not saying much, until I finish.

"Oh, sweetheart, you did give your heart to Phillip. I not only hear it in your words and tears, but I see it in your eyes," she says softly.

"Yes," I say, reaching for a tissue off the nightstand and blowing my nose. "I never let anyone in for this reason. I saw what Aunt Emily went through, and I thought of Dad, and I was too afraid to let anyone in. But maybe I didn't let anyone in before because they weren't Phillip."

"You let him in because you knew it was worth it," Mom

says softly. "When you spoke of your father and him allowing himself to love again—you said that because you knew it was the truth. You were protecting yourself, but you knew when it was right to lower those walls. Phillip is the right man."

"But he doesn't think he's worth it," I reply, my voice shaking.

My mother's pale blue eyes flicker with determination at me. "Then you make him see that he is."

"But how?"

"I think there is more to this story, more that you didn't sort through because of the emotional state you were both in," Mom says firmly. "You said he mentioned debating telling his father, if he would understand. McKenna, think about that comment. I wonder if he's taking on all this responsibility, down to parenting his youngest sister, because his father is unable to. Not unwilling, but unable."

I gasp at her words. What if his father is physically sick or mentally ill? Is this why Phillip has guarded everything so closely and taken on so much? And kept everything secret from even Rose and John?

"Oh, my God," I whisper.

"There is more to this, I know it," Mom says with conviction. "And this young man has taken this all upon himself. He doesn't want to drag you into it out of some kind of misguided good intention. You told him you understand messy—but you need to *convince* him of that. Get the whole story out of him. Make him understand that he can't protect his sisters forever. That they need to be told the truth and held accountable for their own actions. You tell Phillip you will walk with him through any season he weathers as long as he will let you."

"But Mom, I told him I'd never trust him with my heart

again."

"And he told you to forget this ever happened," she says bluntly. "McKenna, my sweet girl, people say all kinds of things when they're hurt and upset. I guarantee you he didn't mean that any more than you meant what you said."

Hope begins to fill me. "Mom, do you really think so?"

"I know so," she says firmly. "He's had time to think just like you did. And if he's half the man you told me he is, I know he regrets this more than anything."

I take a moment to gather myself before speaking. "I know in my heart Anna led me to find Phillip," I say, my voice breaking. "But Mom, you're the one who is going to give him back to me. He's my gift from the both of you—my mum and my mom."

Mom grows emotional in front of my eyes. "Then I can't think of a better man for you than Phillip. Now go make this right."

I thank her and get off the phone. I scramble off the bed and jerk open my dresser drawers, retrieving a navy T-shirt and jeans. I change, quickly brush my teeth, and run a brush through my hair. I need to think. How do I get to Phillip? The last time he withdrew, he stayed far away from me. I'm going to have to go to him, and I'm going to have to surprise him. If I text him or call him and ask to see him, he won't permit it. That's his wall I have to break through.

I draw a breath of air. I'm going to have to ask Rose for her help. I need to find out where he lives in Mayfair so I can go to him.

I check the time. It's still early, so she won't be up for a while. I should eat, but I can't. Probably the worst thing I can do is have a cup of coffee, but there's not much else to do, so I head downstairs.

When I reach the kitchen, I'm stunned to see the lights are on and Rose and John are sitting at the island, drinking coffee and talking softly.

Oh, God. Do they know about Phillip and me? I'm about to turn and run when John spots me.

"You aren't disturbing us, come on in," he says, smiling warmly at me. "Have a seat."

Rose turns in my direction. Her face looks weary. Fear sweeps over me. She knows. But what did Phillip tell her? Is she worried about Georgina? Upset with me? I have no idea what her face is telling me right now.

"Good morning," I manage to say as I take a seat next to Rose.

She coughs lightly. "I talked to Phillip last night."

I look at her. Her eyes are full of sadness.

"He told me what happened with Georgina," she says slowly. "And you."

I blink to force back tears. "I didn't mean what I said to him."

"You were right about a lot of it. He can't keep taking everything on. Georgina is going to have to grow up. I am, too."

I don't say a word. I practically hold my breath and wait for her to continue.

"Phillip is so good with running things, it was easier to let him do everything," she says. "At least, that's what I told myself. All I had to do was complain when I couldn't get what I wanted."

She blushes with shame. John reaches across the island and holds her hand.

"But he's not going to pay the price for everything with the rest of his life," she says resolutely. "John and I will be stepping in with Georgina. We're also going to help him in whatever way he sees fit with running the estates. Now, he's the expert in that, so I don't know how we can help, but we are here for him."

"I'm going to oversee the Italian property," John says. "Phillip agreed to that."

There's a missing piece of the puzzle here with his parents, but I don't dare ask Rose about it. Phillip will have to explain that to me. But all of these changes are huge for him. Something shook him to make him let these things go, to even share the burden with Rose.

"You're the reason he's changing," Rose says, reading my mind. "But he's certain he's lost you."

"No," I cry, "he's wrong about that."

Rose and John exchange a look.

"I said things out of my own past hurts," I say, my voice quivering. "But they aren't true."

"Would you trust Phillip with your heart again?" she asks gently.

"Yes. I want that more than anything, to put my heart in his hands again."

"Good, we were hoping you would say that," John says, his eyes shining brightly at me.

"Go upstairs and pack a bag," Rose says. "I know a certain someone is heading out to Northamptonshire today. And I have a sudden desire to go to Mooreton House for another visit. John, you can work remotely from there this week, can't you?"

"I absolutely can, my love," he says.

I realize what is being said.

Phillip is at Mooreton House.

And they are taking me there to find him.

* * *

The ride out to the country is unbearably long this time. First, it seemed to take forever to get the kids up, dressed, fed, and packed up—which took even longer because Byron was in a foul mood and not cooperating. The hour and forty-five minute drive has seemed to crawl by. Halfway into our trip to Northamptonshire, it began to rain. Slowly at first, then the skies broke open and poured, slowing us even further.

Now the kids are getting antsy and beginning to bicker, and Rose is tired of hearing it, so, the TV monitors are deployed and we're all watching *Shaun the Sheep.* I keep scrolling through my phone, with no messages from Phillip—not that I expected there would be.

Finally, we pull up to the long drive up to Mooreton House, and I'm spilling over with anxiety. I have to break through to Phillip. I have to tear down his wall as he has torn down mine.

"Look! It's Phillip!" Layla cries, pointing out the window.

Phillip? I quickly turn and look out the window, and sure enough, riding across the lush green grass in the rain is Phillip on top of a massive black horse, galloping at a terrific speed.

"That's his horse," Layla says, turning to me knowingly. "His name is Zeus."

My heart is in my throat as I watch him. Phillip glances over to the car, a look of complete surprise taking over his face when he recognizes it. He slows up on his horse, staring at the Range Rover with his mouth open.

John stops the car, and Phillip quickly pulls up beside us. John lowers his window and shouts over the rain at him. "We needed a change of scenery this week. So we'll be here with the kids and McKenna, but we'll be sure to stay out of your hair!" he says cheerfully.

I hold my breath. Phillip whips his head to look in the backseat, and our eyes meet. His eyes grow wide in shock upon sight of me.

131

I bite my lip to keep from crying. He's about to say something when Rose leans across to speak to him.

"We'll go in and get settled now, don't worry about us," she says.

The rain is pelting off Phillip's riding helmet. The rain slicker he has on is soaking wet. Phillip opens his mouth to speak again, but before he can, John raises the window and drives off.

"There, that should get him running into the house now," John says.

I blink back tears. I pray with all my heart John is right. That Phillip doesn't run away from me, knowing I'm here.

I want him to run to me. I want him to come back.

Where he belongs.

Soon, John has pulled up to the back entrance, and I help get the kids out of the car. Suitcases are unloaded, and since Phillip has cut staff to housekeeping and those working the tours, we get all the bags ourselves.

"I can bring your bag up to your room for you," John offers.

I shake my head. "No, thank you, I've got it."

"Well, go on," Rose says.

"You need to go think," Layla adds solemnly.

Yes. I need to think of how to break through to Phillip.

"Come on, kids, let's go on inside and out of the rain, hurry up!" Rose says.

I pick up my suitcase and head into the house. While Rose herds the kids into the kitchen for a snack, I slip up the stairs and head to my room on the children's floor. I glance at the door to Phillip's room, which is open. I swallow hard. I know he's not back yet, but I don't know if he will be coming to find me. He might make plans to leave now that I'm here.

And I can't let that happen.

I take my suitcase to my room, parking it next to the door. I turn around and hurry back down the hall, determined to get to the stables. I'm about to go straight there when I catch sight of the painting at the end of the hall.

Of Phillip's past.

I walk to it, tears welling in my eyes as I stare at the mirror image of the man I'm falling in love with. Phillip's destiny was always here, in this house, in these halls. This Phillip in the painting—the Earl of Castleton—saved it once, and now it has fallen upon the broad shoulders of my Phillip to save the Coventry family once again.

But unlike Phillip, the Earl of Castleton, my Phillip is not going to bear this alone. Not anymore. He has Rose and John to help.

And he will have me.

He'll always have me if he can let me in. If he can allow himself to believe that he is what I want, what I deserve, that I choose him baggage and messiness and all, and no other man will do.

I hear footsteps running up the stairs. I whirl around and find Phillip flying up them, still dressed in his rain slicker and waterproof riding boots.

My heart roars in my ears. I begin to shake. Phillip looks up and stops dead in his tracks when he sees me at the end of the corridor.

I can't speak over the icy wedge that has lodged in my throat. Phillip runs up the rest of the stairs and rushes straight toward me.

I crumble. I can't move, but I don't have to. Phillip runs right to me, and before I can even speak, his mouth crashes down onto mine.

It's a kiss of fire and passion and branding. His mouth is hot and needy. I'm crying, but I kiss him back fiercely, as I know

133

this kiss and what it means.

The walls that were erected between us have been destroyed with this kiss.

I cling to him, desperate for more. My tears mix with the rain on his face. I embrace the scent of his cologne combined with leather and the scent of his horse, and as our tongues collide in desperate desire, I know this is a kiss of forever. His stubble burns against my face, and my fingers tangle in his wet hair. This man is now mine. For now, for always—and forever.

Phillip breaks the kiss and holds my face in his hands. We're both breathing hard and clinging to each other.

"I'm a bloody idiot," Phillip blurts out. "My God, what I said to you. I didn't mean it. I don't want it. I want you. I need you, McKenna. I don't want this life anymore. I want a life with you."

"I want the same thing," I say, grabbing the lapels of his rain slicker and holding on tight. "I want you in my life. I want to see where this goes. I want all the good and the bad and the ugly."

He blinks rapidly. I can tell he's trying to fight back tears.

"When you left me," he says, his voice uneven, "you took my heart. But you woke me up. I can't keep up this charade anymore."

"What charade?" I ask, lifting a hand to his face and caressing his cheek. "Tell me."

He swallows hard. "My father has dementia."

"Oh, God, Phillip," I gasp. "No."

"He asked me to keep it a secret from Rose and Georgina," Phillip says, his voice thick. "But I can't keep all of this up. I can't keep Georgina out of trouble, which ... which is what he made me promise I would do."

Suddenly, it all makes sense. Why he kept all this silent. Why he trailed Georgina at nightclubs, sacrificing his own happiness to do so.

To keep his word.

"You are the most honorable man I've ever met," I whisper, my voice cracking. "But you deserve a life of your own. Georgina needs to know the truth and learn to be an adult. That's not a promise you can keep, and it wasn't a fair one to ask."

He nods. "I know. You made me see that. You made me see so much, McKenna. I ... I'm already falling in love with you."

Happy tears spill from my eyes at his words. "I'm falling in love with you, too. And Phillip, I do trust you with my heart. I do. I said that when I was hurt, but you are the only man who could make me lower my walls. You make me want to be vulnerable. To be open to being hurt because that means I can find love. And I only want to find that with you."

Phillip's eyes become rimmed with red. He wipes away my tears with his calloused fingertips and clears his throat. "I'm so grateful you can forgive me. So grateful."

"I'm grateful you can forgive me, too," I say.

He takes a moment to press a gentle kiss on my lips, then he stands back up. "I've told Rose and John about Dad. She wasn't happy I kept it from her, but she said she's never tried to pull her weight, and she will now. And I believe her."

"I believe her, too."

"My mother is upset, but I know she has a lot going on trying to deal with Dad's illness. It's getting worse now, and decisions will have to be made. But they need to be made by all of us, as a family."

"The way it should be," I say gently.

Phillip gives me a wry smile. "Well, I'm still going to oversee Mooreton House—this is my baby, and I'm not ready to give that up. Or have forty housekeepers, which is what I'm sure Rose would prefer if she was in charge," he teases.

I laugh. "I think that's wise. And you love it here. You need to oversee it."

"I'm going to let John manage the Italian property for my parents, and he and I will jointly manage Montpelier Square. He said he always wanted to help, but Rose always insisted that since they were all going to be my properties, I should run them myself, and they shouldn't interfere."

I nod, seeing how that could be Rose's line of thinking.

"So that is settled now, but there's one piece left to sort out, and that's you," Phillip says, gazing down into my eyes with such tenderness, my heart nearly bursts. "McKenna, I need to hear you say it. Are you willing to take me on?"

I smile up at him with all the love that is forming in my heart for this man. "I am so willing to take you on, *Your Lord Grace Viscount.*"

He throws his head back and laughs deeply.

"Never stop calling me that," he murmurs.

And as his mouth claims mine for another kiss, I vow I never will.

Epilogue

It's a beautiful day for polo in Wokingham, Berkshire, on this sunny July Sunday. I study the field from behind my sunglasses, watching as Phillip thunders across the field on a beautiful gray horse. Today, he's playing in a charity tournament for the House of Chadwick Charities, wearing the royal purple and white jersey for Prince Alexander's team, and playing against Prince Christian, the new Duke of Oxford, and his team.

I've attended a few of Phillip's matches this summer, and I'm getting better at understanding the game. At first, it terrified me, seeing the thundering horses and how close they got together. I was so afraid Phillip would get hurt! But Phillip assured me he knew what he was doing. And he wasn't lying when he said he was a good player—he's easily the best player on the field, and the fact that he is player number 3 means he's the highest-handicapped player. He explained to me that he's the most accurate hitter and best passer. He's the one who is the captain, shouting out orders to his teammates.

We're in the sixth chukker of the game—period of play, I have learned—and Xander's team is in the lead, with a score of seven to the duke's team with six-and-a-half. I'm sitting on a lush green lawn overlooking the field with Rose and the children, who are busy eating ice cream as they wait for the match to end.

Oh, and sitting on my right? Poppy Davies, the girlfriend of Xander Wales, and Her Royal Highness the Duchess of Oxford, Clementine Jones. Both women have engaged me in conversation since Phillip introduced them to me before the match began.

I nearly laugh out loud. If I hadn't had nothing but water this afternoon, I would swear I was drunk. Of course, the constant pictures being snapped of two of the most photographed women in the world kind of served as a massive reality check as well.

Once I got past that moment of being starstruck, I discovered each woman was friendly, normal, and down-to-earth. Clementine was thrilled to meet another West Coast American, and we talked a lot about things we love about England—and miss about California. Like wandering through Target. When she found out my background is in early childhood education, she said I had to meet Liz—*as in Her Royal Highness Princess Elizabeth of York*—as that is one of her core causes. I could hardly believe it. And I was gobsmacked when Clementine put her contact information into my phone.

Byron walks up to me, interrupting my thoughts about this surreal day. "Would you like a bite of my ice cream?" he asks.

I beam at him. We've come a long way since I didn't know who the farmer was on *Shaun the Sheep.*

"I would love one," I say, smiling at him.

He dips his cone toward me, and I take a bite of it. "Mm! That is so good. Thank you so much for sharing that with me."

"You're welcome," he says, then he moves back over to his seat next to Rose.

Rose leans in to whisper in my ear. "I know this makes me a terrible person, but I am utterly delighted that you are getting dagger looks from Lady India Rothschild."

"What? Why?" I ask, wondering why on earth India would despise me.

"She had her sights set on Xander earlier this year. I know you aren't a big royal follower, but you will become one now that you are part of the circle that moves within theirs. Anyway, when that didn't pan out, she set her sights on Phillip."

"What?" I gasp. "Really?"

I can't help it. I glance down the lawn, where I see India—dressed to kill in a gorgeous designer sundress—is staring at me with a look of disgust on her beautiful face.

"Oh God, yes. Made cow eyes at him when he was at the clubs watching Georgina. Texted him constantly. Flirted like mad with him. But obviously, we know she is not his type and that my scowling brother with a heart of gold has a thing for a certain California girl with an equal heart of gold."

I blush, and she laughs.

"I imagine India can't believe he chose the nanny over her," I muse.

Rose snorts. "Anyone who has met the horrid woman can believe it!"

I can't help it. I laugh, and Rose does, too.

My eyes return to the field, finding Phillip in command, directing his team and passing the ball to Xander. I have never been in love before, and it is the greatest feeling in the world, to love Phillip—and to have him love me back in the same way.

We fell in love quickly, but I've never doubted it. And one morning, at the end of June, when he took me to watch the sun rise over St. Paul's Cathedral, he told me he was grateful to Anna for bringing me to him, and to my mom, Samantha, for making me the woman he loved with all his heart. I began to ugly cry—of course—and proclaimed there was nobody I was destined to love except for him.

And in front of St. Paul's, we talked of our future. Of getting married someday and moving to Northamptonshire on a permanent basis. I am going to stay on as his sister's nanny until then, and when the triplets start school in the fall, I'm going to work on some online courses toward a master's degree in early childhood studies, which I'm super excited about.

"I know Xander and Christian fought over who got Phillip on their team," Poppy says, interrupting my thoughts. "And now I see why."

I smile proudly. "Phillip is rather good, isn't he?"

Clementine laughs. "Christian already declared him for their next charity tournament in September," she says.

My heart flutters as I watch Phillip on his horse. He's been teaching me how to ride, and we spent a lot of weekends in Northamptonshire doing just that. Enjoying the outdoors, riding, and embracing the life he has been given—a life that has become ours. Phillip stays in London during the week, and we see each other nearly every day, which makes both of us happy.

John has been a tremendous help to Phillip in taking over the Italian estate. Lady Georgina, after throwing fits and many bouts of tears, has been cut off from extra funding. The nude pictures did make headlines, but as with anything in a news cycle, they have died down now. Phillip—with Rose by his side—has held firm with her, and while their relationship is suffering, I know he's doing the right thing. Not just for him, but for her, too. She has to grow up. And now is her chance to do so.

As far as my family goes, I keep in touch with Grace and my cousins, mostly via text these days. It's still a new friendship we all have, and I'm not sure where it will go, but we're all keeping the doors open for it to grow. My parents are coming for a visit at the end of September, and I'm so excited to introduce them to Phillip and our London that we've discovered together.

The game comes to an end, and Phillip has led Xander's team to victory. There's a trophy presentation to come, but for now, Phillip comes across the field, flanked by Xander, Christian, and another friend of Phillip's I met earlier, a ginger-haired man named Charlie.

God, is there anything sexier than Phillip in his polo uniform? The boots, the white jeans that hug his massive legs, the sunglasses on, the leather gloves, carrying his mallet as he laughs at something Christian has said ... Oh, yes, today is warm, but I think the temperature is going up with each step he takes closer to me.

Soon he's before me, and my heart bursts with pride. He removes his glasses, and we all congratulate the winning players—while Clementine consoles Christian and Charlie, who were on the losing side of things.

Phillip has spoken of Charlie before, and with both of them in the unique position of inheriting large estates, it's something that has bonded them together. During the past month, Phillip has reached out to him for advice, and to his surprise, Charlie confided in him some difficulties he has inherited with his estates, too. Ones far deeper rooted and harder to dig out of than what Phillip was dealt.

Yet despite this, Charlie is before me, grinning and laughing and calling Phillip a traitor for playing for Xander, and I can't help but hope he finds his way like Phillip is finding his.

"I think this calls for dinner out this evening," Xander says, spinning his mallet in his hand.

"Only if the winner picks up the tab," Christian says, shooting him a cheeky grin.

"In honor of all the money raised for our charities today, I will gladly pick up the tab," Xander declares. He turns to Phillip. "Are you in, captain?"

Phillip glances at me. "Depends on what McKenna wants to do. What do you think, love?"

I beam at him. "I'm in."

"See? She knows not to turn down a free meal," Phillip says dryly.

We all laugh. Xander makes plans for us to all meet at some gourmet burger place, and soon the winning team has to get ready to go get their trophy. Xander and Christian head off with Charlie, but Phillip lingers behind for a moment, stepping closer to me and setting butterflies off in my stomach, as he always seems to do.

He moves his hands to my waist. Phillip is an intoxicating blend of sweat, grass, and leather, and his lips briefly meet mine for a sweet kiss.

"I love you," he murmurs.

"And I love you, Lord Grace Viscount," I murmur against his mouth.

He chuckles against my lips and lifts his head.

Phillip grins at me. "Don't ever stop saying that."

Then he turns and runs to catch up with his teammates for the cup presentation.

I smile as I watch him, this man who rescued me in a cow pasture and helped me find myself. My heart.

And most of all, love.

No, my love, I think as I watch him. *I'll always call you Lord Grace Viscount.*

And I will do so for the rest of my life.

THE END

To keep up with news and release information for other books in the Modern Aristocrat series, please sign up for my newsletter at www.avenellis.com. You can also join my reader group, *Kate, Skates, and Coffee Cakes,* on Facebook.

About the Author

Aven began her publishing career in 2013 with her debut release, *Connectivity*. She currently writes British billionaires, royals, hockey and baseball romantic comedies.

Her books are designed to make readers laugh out loud and fall in love. Happily-ever-after endings and good-boy heroes are guaranteed.

Aven lives in the Dallas area with her family. She is a huge fan of both the Dallas Stars and Texas Rangers. Aven loves shopping and fashion and can spend hours playing with fragrances in any department store. She can be found chatting it up on social media, eating specialty M&Ms, and crushing on the latest outfit the Duchess of Cambridge is wearing.

You can connect with me on:
- http://avenellis.com
- https://twitter.com/AvenEllis
- https://www.facebook.com/AuthorAvenEllis
- https://www.instagram.com/avenellis

Also by Aven Ellis

If you enjoyed this book, please check out some of my other romantic comedies:

Connectivity (British Isles Billionaires #1).
  Connectivity 2.0 (British Isles Billionaires #2).
  A Royal Shade of Blue (Modern Royals #1)
  The Princess Pose (Modern Royals #2)
  Royal Icing (Modern Royals #3).
  Squeeze Play (Washington DC Soaring Eagles #1)
  Swing and a Miss (Washington DC Soaring Eagles #2).
 A Complete Game (Washington DC Soaring Eagles #3)
 Hold the Lift (Rinkside in the Rockies Novella)
 Sugar and Ice (Rinkside in the Rockies #1)
 Reality Blurred (Rinkside in the Rockies #2)
 Outscored (Rinkside in the Rockies #3)
 Home Ice (Dallas Demons #1)
 The Definition of Icing (Dallas Demons #2)
 Breakout (Dallas Demons #3)
 On Thin Ice (Dallas Demons #4)
 Playing Defense (Dallas Demons #5)
 The Aubrey Rules (Chicago on Ice #1)
 Trivial Pursuits (Chicago on Ice #2)
 Save the Date (Chicago on Ice #3)
 The Bottom Line (Chicago on Ice #4)

Made in the USA
Monee, IL
02 June 2021